REIGN OF RUIN

Jennifer Bene

Text copyright © 2019 Jennifer Bene

All Rights Reserved

No part of this book may be reproduced in any form or by any electronic or mechanical means including information storage and retrieval systems, without permission in writing from the author. The only exception is by a reviewer, who may quote short excerpts in a review.

This book is a work of fiction. Names, characters, places, and incidents either are products of the author's imagination or are used fictitiously. Any resemblance to actual persons, living or dead, events, or locales is entirely coincidental.

ISBN (e-book): 978-1-946722-40-9

ISBN (paperback): 978-1-946722-41-6

Cover design by Laura Hidalgo, Beyond DEF Lit. https://www.beyonddeflit.com/

❦ Created with Vellum

FOREWORD

"I no longer had a taste for anything, a wish for anything, a love for anybody, a desire for anything whatever, any ambition, or any hope."

— *Guy de Maupassant*

This book originally appeared as 'Baptized in Eden' in the Twisted Sacrament anthology where various sacraments were run through a dark romance / horror filter. I got to do that anthology with some of my favorite wicked-minded ladies, and the stories that came from it were all much closer to the horror end of the pool than dark romance! (insert evil laugh here)

So, here is your warning, lovelies. While 'Reign of Ruin' has over 20,000 words added to it through an extended epilogue, and a bonus short story at the end… it's still dark af. This is not one of those happy ending, everything-turns-out-okay kind of books. Similar to Breaking Beth, this is a walk deeper

FOREWORD

and deeper into a dark cave where all that lies at the end is an empty darkness. I will say that this time there is a certain element of righteous vengeance, but I'll leave you to decide if you think Danielle should be happy or not.

Still, even with all the deep dark insanity inside these pages, I do hope that you'll give it a chance. It's wicked, dirty, and (hopefully) the beginning of more books in this fucked up world my mind created.

Be sure to read all the way to the end, because there's a fantastic short story titled 'The Day the Sky Burned' that I wrote to help readers understand (a bit) how the world ended up so spectacularly fucked up.

Enjoy the journey, lovelies!

Jennifer Bene

CHAPTER 1

"Light thinks it travels faster than anything but it is wrong. No matter how fast light travels, it finds the darkness has always got there first, and is waiting for it."

— Terry Pratchett

Waking was a painful thing. Joints creaking, headache like an ice pick through her temple, but Danielle still lifted herself upright if only to ease the ache in her shoulders. Something held her arms above her head, elbows near her hairline… and there were others around her.

People breathing.

Someone crying quietly.

Another whispering in a language she didn't recognize, but she would have sworn on a Bible it was a prayer.

"You awake?" a voice asked from her right, and she twisted to look through hazy eyes... or maybe it was the room that was hazy. The air thick, gray.

"*What?*" It came out raspy, weak. Mouth sticky, throat struggling to scratch out the word.

"Finally. I was wondering if you were gone for good." There was a soft huff, and Danielle blinked hard to clear the murk from her gaze, focusing hard on the shape beside her even though she felt half-asleep.

"Wha—" She scraped her feet over the grit on the floor, feeling more of it shift under her thighs, her ass. *Naked?* "Where am I? What happened?"

"Don't remember?" It was a woman, a tired but feminine voice, and slowly her features were framed in the meager light. Long, pale hair hanging around a sharp face.

"No, I—" Swallowing against her dry throat, she tried to form thoughts that didn't want to align, like pressing together the wrong puzzle pieces... nothing fit. "Where am I? I'm not supposed to be here. I need to go. *Please.*"

"You must have come from somewhere nice."

"Huh?" Head still fogged, Danielle shook it, and the sound of chain shook with her. "What do you mean?"

"You still think you'll be saved, you still have hope. Most don't even think getting out is an option anymore. That's... unique. They'll like that because it's something else they can take."

"Who? What are you talking about? Where are we?" Questions tumbled from her faster than her mind could process, and the woman beside her just stared with dead eyes. Empty. Her skin sallow and cheeks hollowed.

"No memories yet?" she asked, ignoring all of Danielle's questions.

Raking through the distorted fog of her mind she saw clips and slices of a life that didn't involve this dingy room, or the soft whimpers of women, or the dull clanking of chains in the dim. "I don't understand."

"They woke you up because they wanted to... because they wanted *you*." An answer that was not an answer. Not helpful.

"What do you mean? What is this?"

"They call it Eden, but I call it Hell."

"What? No..." Danielle jerked at the chains again, feeling the ache in her wrists that warned her against it, but panic was rising from the confusion, a bright strike of fear in the murk. "I don't know how I got here, but this has to be a mistake. It's a mistake, I'm not supposed to be here, I'm supposed to be—"

Where was she supposed to be?

The information slipped from her like water through fingers. Almost there, almost caught, but lost before she could get it to her lips. To swallow it, to know it, to think it, to speak it.

"Home?" the woman offered, a slight flick of her eyebrow and a quirk of her lip clearly making a mockery of the word that should have held comfort.

"Yes."

"I had a home, a husband before all this. I had a child, a daughter. She was young, although I still can't remember how old she was, but... I think they died, which is for the best. I wouldn't want them here. There is no home for any of us anymore."

Danielle swallowed, turning her eyes up to the thick ring buried in the wall, following the chains down to the thick manacles on her wrists. Old fashioned, the kinds of things you'd see in a museum exhibit on torture.

No one expects the Spanish Inquisition.

The phrase erupted from her mind, almost made her smile, mouth quirking at the edges like she should laugh, but it all festered into confusion, a muddling fear that the woman beside her would wish her child dead rather than here.

Here, where Danielle was.

"Did I have a family?" she asked, worried about the answer, but still desperate for the knowledge.

"How would I know?" Another mocking glance as the woman shuffled herself back against the wall, swinging her bound arms to one side to lean closer, whispering like a confidant. "You'll remember almost everything eventually."

"I don't remember," Danielle insisted. "I don't remember anything."

"I know. I know you don't. You should enjoy the quiet." The woman nodded, head lolling back against the wall where her face was obscured by her arms, but her voice whispered out into the gloom, promising damnation. "Once you remember you won't be able to think of anything else."

CHAPTER 2

"Name?" the man asked, but she was frozen just inside the door.

Well, frozen except for the shudders making her muscles twitch.

Fear. Pure and refined by this *hell* was moving through her veins. The woman had been right. She'd been right about everything... but Danielle hadn't seen her for weeks. Or had it been a month? More?

Maybe she'd died. Escaped to join her family in the peace that would come after the last beat of her heart. Enough of them begged for it that death didn't even seem bad anymore, but this man sitting in the chair, one arm draped over the side like a throne — he was bad.

Evil.

Hungry.

A laugh rolled out of him, so low and sinister that she

expected it to be followed by black smoke. Expected his eyes to turn red, glowing like a devil, but he was human.

They were all just people.

Somehow that made it worse.

"Your name doesn't really matter." Snapping his fingers, he pointed at the floor. "Come here."

Danielle walked forward in slow, padding steps. Obeying, barely, stretching out the time before the pain, the screaming. When she ran out of room, she stared down at his boots. Mud-speckled and thick-soled.

"Knees."

Her body folded like a marionette with its strings cut. Graceless, she didn't even flinch when the impact of the kneel echoed up her bones.

"So pretty. So fresh." Grabbing her face with a calloused hand, he squeezed her jaw, brushing the dry pad of his thumb over her mouth. He plucked at her lower lip, traced her teeth, lifted her chin so she was looking at him. "I think I do want your name."

"Danielle," she whispered and then his thumb was in her mouth, bent over her teeth to press into the soft place under her tongue, digging in. Hard. His fingers under her chin did the same, nails threatening to pierce flesh as if he wanted them to meet. To rip her open. A guttural sound escaped her and he groaned, hauling her forward by the painful hold until she knelt between his legs.

"*Danielle*," he repeated, but from his lips it sounded like a threat. Emphasized by the torment of his thumb burrowing deeper into pooling saliva, thumbnail adding copper to the tang of fear. Her tongue curled away from the pain, seeking refuge against the roof of her mouth. A coward.

Drool dripped. Fists clenched. Pain faded as she grew used to it, but his eyes were on hers. A dull blue, like old paint. Sun-bleached and rotting. His face was tanned, weather worn, wild. The brown of his close-cropped beard run through with strands of amber when he tilted his face and it caught the light.

He was older than her, by twenty years or so, but the body under his clothes was all strength. Battle-hardened and brutal, and the bulge behind the buttons of his pants matched his size.

Tall, powerful, *male*.

This was going to hurt. A lot.

He leaned forward, the bulk of his shoulders blocking some of the light until he was a dark shadow framed in a yellow haze. "I'm going to fuck this pretty mouth of yours"—his fingers dug in just a little harder and she couldn't stifle the whimper, a garbled, incomplete plea—"and then I'm going to make you scream before I fuck you into a bloody puddle."

Those words burrowed deeper than the fingers bruising her.

Those words were promises.

Tears burned the edges of her eyes as he eased off the pressure with his thumb, only to trace the drool over her top lip and then smear it across her cheek. In another life she would have begged, called out for help, run for the door — but she'd tried all those things on other nights.

Begging made them happy.

Calling out made them hurt her worse.

And the door was always, *always*, locked the moment she was pushed inside.

So, Danielle stayed on her throbbing knees as he sat up in the chair. Swallowed the drool left in her mouth. Traced the sore place he'd left behind with the tip of her tongue, unable to stop prodding even when it stung. Even when she tasted the blood he'd drawn.

Looking up at him, he seemed taller, larger from the perspective, and then a new flash of memory hit her.

The warmth of a fire. A soothing voice reading a book aloud. Her fingers working at a braid. Her sister's braid, her father's voice, the smell of real food cooking.

As quickly as it had come, it was gone, and it left her colder than before. The loss of people she couldn't even name hollowing out a place inside her chest as if the scraps of her heart were trying to escape with sharpened spoons.

How fucked was it to remember something good while she was naked and kneeling before a goddamned monster? A monster that was going to fuck her. That was a promise made by his presence in this room, in this place. *Hell.*

His fingers wound around her throat, squeezing, as the other hand popped the buttons on his pants one at a time. When his cock came free, pants adjusted to let it stand tall, Danielle tried to coat her lips and tongue with the drool he'd summoned.

Anything to make it easier.

"Hands behind your back. If you move them, you know what'll happen." It was a casual command, so little effort behind it because he knew it would be obeyed — and she did obey. Clasping one hand around the opposite wrist, she waited as his fingers wormed their way into her hair, gathering it on either side of her head to keep it out of the way as he pulled her forward.

Drawing the head of his cock between her lips didn't require a command.

Refusing the urge to bite didn't require a threat.

Danielle dipped her head down voluntarily, and laved the underside of his shaft with her tongue before she sealed her lips to his flesh. His guttural groan was a triumph, and she ignored the tender space in her mouth so that she could focus on pleasing him.

When they were happy, they weren't so violent.

Usually.

But something about this man, something in the dull glint of his blue eyes, or the calm tone of his powerful voice, told her that he was going to hurt her no matter how well she sucked his cock. It wouldn't matter if he came down her throat, wouldn't matter if she hummed a moan when her lips were pressed to the base of him. There would be pain. But, for a single moment, she tried to determine if she was still concerned about dying, wondered if her self-preservation had dissolved enough to join the other wraiths that walked these halls waiting for their chance to be free.

It was just a moment though.

His fingers tightened in her hair, the sting of strands ripping free of her scalp preceding his first harsh thrust into her throat. Yanked forward, nose buried into the fabric of his shirt, she pressed ragged nails into her skin to keep her hands still. Swallowing around the girth forced past the point where air could slip by, Danielle tried to accept it. To wait for the moment when his own needs would force him to move, to seek more friction — the moment when she'd be able to breathe.

Throat convulsing, stomach heaving, she finally got a sip of air before she choked on the next thrust. The hot tears in her eyes were a biological response to the gagging, the lack of air, not an emotional one. She'd cried all the tears she could before now. Used all the words she knew to beg and plead, and not a single person had cared.

She was an object. A warm body to be used.

And she still couldn't remember how the fuck she'd ended up here.

He was bruising her throat, making flashes of light beat behind clenched eyelids to the pounding of her pulse as he deprived her of air. Wet, desperate gasps were all she could catch on the few thrusts that pulled him out of her throat. Just enough to keep her conscious, to keep her mouth and tongue working on him, even if most of it now was automatic convulsions.

The only conscious effort was keeping her lips folded over her teeth as best she could. Another fruitless attempt to ease the pain she knew was coming. *This?* This relentless fucking of her throat, the pounding of his cock between her lips, the harsh grunts above her buzzing ears? It was nothing. It was easy. If this was all he wanted from her, she'd lick his fucking boots clean in appreciation.

"Take it," he growled and forced her down once again. Nose buried against fabric she couldn't smell because she couldn't breathe. The urge to pull back, to brace her hands against his knees and push, to bite down and force her way to air… it was all-consuming. Every neuron in her brain fired at once demanding oxygen.

'BREATHE,' her body shouted, commanded, and the death grip of her nails on her wrist eased, violence rising in her head like a red haze from a lizard-brain that only knew death or survival.

But then he moved again, a fraction of air making its way to her lungs, just enough to return sanity and allow her to switch the grip behind her back. Opposite hand now, pressing jagged nails into skin to remind her of the things they'd done to teach her not to bite. Not to fight.

Male skin slicked over her tongue, drool pooling to ease his path, welcoming him into her throat before his next long withdrawal spilled it down her chin and graced her with oxygen in the same movement.

His thrusts grew shorter, quicker, and she tried to focus and suck him, moving her tongue with purpose, stroking, urging him to completion as she made herself drunk on the air whistling in and out of her nose.

"*Fuck!*" The word spat out as he pushed deep, tightening his grip in her hair, cock pulsing in her throat as he came in twitching jerks, only able to taste him when he finally eased back. Appeased for a moment, hands still wound in her hair but no longer painful.

A fleeting reprieve.

She gentled the movement of her tongue against his

softening flesh, swallowed again and again in an aching throat as he pulled his hips back, letting her mouth play with the flared head for a second or two longer — but that was all he gave her.

When he pulled himself free and wrenched her head backwards, she tried to avoid his eyes, but they filled the full frame of her vision and she knew closing her eyelids would only make him angry. Danielle couldn't have described herself in that moment, couldn't remember a time before this place where she might have done this for someone who cared about her.

At least she knew how to suck cock.

Like riding a bike… even though she couldn't quite remember if she'd ever ridden one.

One hand released her hair, a thumb plucking at her lips again as he smiled. "I've missed that," he hummed, tilting his head a little as he smeared more drool and traces of his seed across her chin. "Tell me, do you scream as well as you whine around a cock in your throat?"

Had she whined? It had been unconscious if she had, but she knew he didn't really want an answer.

"Will you scream for me?" His fingers tightened on her chin, and she nodded. No use in lying. "Speak."

He actually wanted her to answer?

It took a hard swallow to make her voice work, but she finally forced out a whispered, "Yes, sir."

A groan left him, and his fist ripped her head back further by her hair, the sting spreading fast across her scalp to meet the ache in her neck. Then he leaned forward to hover his face above hers. "Say it again."

"Yes, sir."

"Nice," he growled and then shoved her backward by the grip on her chin. She caught herself on one elbow, wondering if he was done with her, but it didn't last as he stood and grabbed her other arm in a rough grip. Without a word, he dragged her over the floor. Knees, shins, feet scraped against the rough wood, helpless sounds dripping from her bruised lips as she tried not to fight.

Fighting makes it worse.

Fighting makes them hit you first.

She may not have the memories of her life back, but her memories of Eden were complete, and getting kicked in the ribs wasn't something you forgot easily. Nor was a hard slap, or the impact of a fist into the soft, yielding flesh of an empty belly.

When he dropped her to the floor, she caught herself just enough that her face didn't hit, and then she stayed still. Listened, eyes studying the grains in the wood, the tiny pale dot that could have been dust or a piece of lint embedded just beneath her.

"You know what I miss most? From before all of this shit?" His tone was disturbingly conversational, even as she heard the rattle of chain being gathered.

This was one of those times he didn't actually want an answer.

"Coffee. *Fuck*. Do you remember coffee? Cream and sugar with that bitter aftertaste that you still craved day after fucking day?" The man was musing aloud as she cowered on the floor, painstakingly drawing her limbs in inch-by-inch so as not to draw too much attention. Unable to remember the flavor of coffee, even though she knew what it was. The color of it, the look, like a picture from a book. "I used to drink a few cups before I even got dressed. It made it all more bearable. The everyday shit."

Heavy boots moved closer and she flinched, one leg jerking upward to protect her belly, chin tucking against her chest. Still just a pathetic mammal at the core, shielding vital points from a predator.

"I used to think about coffee a lot. Coffee, and fucking." The reinforced toe of his boot pressed against a kidney with a nudge, as if to point out she wasn't safe.

Like she could have forgotten that.

"At least I can still get one fix, right?" Still so conversational, even as he grabbed her hair in a fist and forced her upright. She yelped as he shoved her into the wall, breasts crushed against it until her ribs felt the weight of his hand pushing between her shoulders. "Don't move."

The pressure eased as he moved to her side, wrapping coils of clattering chain around one wrist before securing it and attaching it to the hook high above her head. Danielle was a touch too short for it to be comfortable, and he could have given her another link or two of slack if he'd cared at all, but instead he just repeated the process with her other arm.

On her toes, she already winced at the strain in her calves, the pain of the metal grinding against the bones of her wrists, even though she knew this was nothing.

Knew the second he began gathering her hair up to tie it off that she'd keep her promise to him.

She would scream.

It was the first whisper of leather behind her that made her body jerk. An involuntary reaction, a surge of fear, muscles tensing in preparation, fists clenching.

And then the world distorted with agony, lungs so stunned she made no sound at all as fire ripped across her back and her eyes squeezed so tight she saw flares of purple and green. Another crack of the whip lanced over her shoulder, and she choked on air as she cried out.

"You can do better than that," he taunted, and then he whipped her again, and again, and again, and somewhere in the midst of mind-consuming anguish she had screamed — was still screaming.

Danielle felt her flesh split, legs giving out so that the crush of chain held her aloft, threatening to break her wrists even as the first warm trail of blood marked its way down her back, finding the groove of her spine.

He barely even paused.

Another wicked slash, another scream that tore her throat, more wet spilling down her back. Only aware of it as the air cooled it on her skin. Everything else was pain, brutal and unforgiving as she went limp, as her ears turned the crack of the whip and her own cries to a buzzing hum.

Black was closing in, blacker than the darkness behind closed eyes, and she leaned into it, pleaded for it in the scraps of thought she was capable.

Somewhere she heard the echo of a soothing voice reading aloud, felt the heat of fire instead of the burning lashes, and then she remembered thunder.

But it wasn't thunder.

The booms that shook the floor, rattled the windows, filled the daylight with black smoke... grew louder, came closer, turned into earthquakes, and screaming, and rubble.

∽

"U<small>NGH</small>!" H<small>ER VOICE WAS A GRUNT, GUTTURAL AND CHOKING</small>, but it wasn't because of smoke and dust. It was because he was on top of her, inside her, and the pain in her back was all-consuming as he thrust and rocked her against the coarse sheet. She was awake, just enough to feel everything. Including the throbbing ache between her thighs as he forced her wide, knees bent towards her shoulders. A weak cry left her, and he growled in satisfaction, fucking her harder, grinding her bloody back into the thin mattress so that the pain amplified, crescendoed, and colors swarmed on the insides of her eyelids.

"Stay awake, Danielle. It's so much nicer with you awake." His head lowered, beard scraping against her cheek, her neck, and then she felt his tongue moving warm and wet over her shoulder. The dark was close, this torture too much for consciousness, but he kept talking, words buzzing against her ear. "You feel good... yeah... scream again..."

Teeth clamped down where her neck curved and she did scream, weak and pathetic, body jerking as his jaw tightened, until the pain blurred with the rest of it and she felt her mind wobble. There, and then not, then back for another thrust, and then she was slipping into the dark.

Mouth against hers, tongue invading, teeth nipping her lip sharply — thankfully not enough to pull her out of the slide. Even his words meant nothing in the haze of pain.

"I'm going to keep fucking you until they take you." A hard drive, fingers digging into the tender flesh behind one knee. "A blood-soaked mess, covered in my seed."

Okay. No argument as everything dissolved.

Why would she care what he did with her body?

CHAPTER 3

It was the chill that woke her, the water around her long bereft of its warmth — if it had ever been warm at all. Sometimes the heating vats broke down and there was only frigid water, but at least it was water. Sliding further down the sunken table she dipped her lips into the cool and drank slowly.

Another lesson she'd learned in Eden. Drinking too fast after a baptism only made her choke, vomit, but it still felt good to sate the thirst.

"This one is awake." A male voice that promised more pain if she didn't behave. There were plenty of things they could do to her without leaving a mark. Carefully, she took in a large mouthful of water just before they started to raise the table. She held it on her tongue as the cold water flowed off her, making her even colder as the air hit her skin. The table clicked and jerked until it finally stopped, but she stayed still, letting the liquid trickle down her throat in small swallows.

Not too much. Not too fast.

It would be worthless if she threw it all up, and then they would be angry because they'd have to clean it up. Everything was simpler if she never made mistakes. Not better, but simpler. The man to her right grabbed her shoulder, roughly rolling her onto her side to run a rough hand across her back. "All good. Mark her down."

"Got it," the other man replied, removing the belt across her waist with a flick of his wrist. "Take her to room four."

That rough hand wrapped around her arm, pulling her upright, and she climbed down from the table without being asked. Dripping with water, she shivered. Pinpricks of pain stabbed at her numb feet as she walked stiffly beside the man wearing plain gray clothes.

Out of the baptism baths, into the hall, two doors down. Room four.

The man rapped his knuckles against the wood, his grip adjusting on her arm but not letting go. As if she would run when there was nowhere to run. No real memory of a safe place she might *want* to run toward.

The door opened and she stared at the hem of the priest's robe as he spoke. "Thank you, my child, you may go."

As soon as she was released, Danielle walked into the room and took her place on the chair. Knees together, hands in her lap, head bowed, still shivering, still dripping water onto the floor around her.

This was the most difficult part of it all. The rules within the insanity. It was almost easier when she performed service, because at least then there was no pretty lie over everything. No formality. Just pain and sex. Just a body. Simple.

"God has chosen you to be baptized and reborn again, my child. What do you say?"

"Thank you, God, for your grace and your love." It was a memorized script. One she wasn't even sure the priest in front of her believed, but wrong answers were not allowed.

"How do you give your thanks?" he asked.

"With all of my *self*, father." Danielle's teeth chattered behind lips pressed hard together to keep the sound to herself. Soon she would be on a cot, covered in the thin blanket until they summoned her again. As long as she played her role, she would have a moment to rest.

"Good. Through suffering you may find absolution." He paused, and she could feel his eyes on her as another shiver raced through her muscles. "Now, what do you want, my child?"

To burn this place to the ground.

"To serve in whatever way God needs me to serve," she answered, even though her throat seemed to protest the words and the lie came out tight, strained.

The subtle flicking of paper filled the air for a moment and she worried he'd caught her hesitation, but then he spoke. "Good. You're looking thin, would you like to eat?"

All thoughts of sleeping on a cot disappeared. This was wrong. The next line was, *'Then you shall serve God in Eden until he calls you home.'* None of the priests had ever broken the script before, and how many times had she sat in one of these chairs?

"You may answer, my child."

Is this a trick?

"Yes, father." Of course, she wanted food. She'd felt hunger for so long she barely noticed it anymore. Meals were infrequent, random, and always the same. Gray and grainy and tasteless.

"God wants you healthy in your service to him. I will ensure you are fed." He paused for a long time, but she had no script for this and had learned that silence was always the better choice in this hell. "Are you grateful?"

"Yes. Thank you, father."

"Show me your gratitude." There was a rustle of fabric, and she shivered — but this time it wasn't from the chill on her skin. "Come here, my child."

Standing, she walked forward until she could see plain black shoes peeking out from the bottom of his pants. The robe was open, draped over the sides of his chair, and then she heard the zipper. Her stomach churned, but she knelt. Lifeless, even as his stance widened so she could move between his legs.

"God honors those who serve him." He kept the gentle, docile tone that all of the priests had as his hand rested on top of her wet hair and pulled her head forward.

There were no words for this, no required responses, except to open her mouth and take the man's offered cock. Out of habit, she placed her hands behind her back, grasping one wrist as his hard shaft slipped between her lips and over her tongue. His thumb rubbed back and forth in her hair, almost comforting, only the gentlest nudges guiding her up and down. In many ways, it was relaxing. Easy. He wasn't violent, his flesh was clean and warm, and he moaned occasionally as he whispered Hail Mary prayers into the air above her bobbing head.

"Oh, my Mother, preserve me this day from mortal sin," he prayed, groaning as his hips lifted to push his cock just a little deeper into her mouth. Danielle took the hint, swallowing to move him into her throat. After a moment, she choked and pulled back, but his fingers pressed into her scalp, urging her down. "…pray for us sinners…"

If she'd had enough left inside to laugh, or the bravery to roll her eyes, she would have. Instead, she teased him with her tongue, sucking just a little harder to hear him stumble in the next repetition of the prayers.

"Yes, my child, just like that. God honors"—a shuddered breath and a groan—"he honors those who serve. Yesss…" He gripped the arm of the chair still covered by his robe, and pushed her head down just as he came. The taste of his seed coated her tongue, and she swallowed again and again until there was only the masculine aftertaste and his heavy breaths above her. Clearing his throat, he spoke in a soft voice. "That was a gift, my child. Thank you."

When he removed his hand, she pulled back and shifted to sit on her heels. Just as she settled, he caught her chin and raised her face to look at him. Soft brown eyes in a middle-aged face, cheeks flushed from his efforts. He swiped at the corner of her mouth and then traced a cross on her forehead with the mix of saliva and ejaculate.

"You are blessed to be reborn in such a haven."

"Yes, father," she answered. It seemed to be the only correct response, and his smile — and the lack of a slap across her face — confirmed it.

"Come with me." A command, not a request, so she stood and waited for him to put his softening dick back in his pants and close his robe. Instead of the door to the cots, he led her through the door in the corner behind his desk. It opened to a narrow hall, dimly lit, and as they passed other doors, she knew they must be walking behind the other rooms filled with priests.

How many others had women on their knees showing their gratitude?

The hypocrisy of it all had long lost its humorous appeal, but there were always new levels of sacrilege to discover in Eden. At the end of the hall, there were stairs leading down, just as narrow, and the old wood creaked as they descended. The room at the bottom was large, and it looked older. Three long tables dominated the space with benches on either side and he gestured for her to sit.

Obeying, she took a spot at the closest table, at the end, and kept her eyes glued to the table. Following patterns in the wood until they ended, and she chose a new line of the grain to follow. Then he slid a bowl of soup in front of her. Actual warm soup with tiny vegetables floating in it. Danielle was so enticed, she immediately reached for the spoon resting in it, but was pulled up short by a sharp tug on her hair.

"Thank God for your food."

Salivating, she swallowed a mouthful of drool as she clasped her hands and bowed her head, reciting the prayer he wanted. Another memorized script that meant nothing. It was hard to wait after she finished, knuckles turning white as the seconds ticked by and the steam coming from the bowl started to diminish. Finally, the priest released her hair.

"You may eat, my child."

Danielle attacked the bowl with more interest than she'd shown anything since... well, since she could remember. Not like there was much to remember, but in none of those memories lurked anything as pleasant as the warm broth sliding down her throat. It pushed back the frigid chill in her skin, ebbed the shivers, and she didn't even care that there was no real taste to it. Bland, simple, but by far the best thing she'd swallowed in Eden.

As she savored the soup, letting each spoonful fill her mouth before she ate it, the vegetables too soft to even chew, a new memory surfaced.

Bright sunlight, green grass, a café. A young, handsome man smiling at her as he reached over the metal lattice of the table top to grasp her hand. His lips moved, but there was no sound, no voice, just a playful grin and a silent laugh.

Then it was gone, taking the kind face and the feeling of safety with it, leaving her with only a meager spoonful of broth. The shallow bowl had emptied too quickly. Her spoon scraped along the ceramic as she gently tilted it to try and get the last few drops without lifting the actual dish to her lips. Before she could get the last tiny spoonful, the priest plucked both items from her hands. "Continue to serve God, and you may earn more."

Nodding, accepting, she tried to focus on the feeling of warmth in her belly where it gurgled and rumbled, as desperate for the food as she had been. For once she was actually grateful when she said, "Thank you, father."

He smiled at her, setting the bowl and spoon on a counter beside an old stovetop. A large pot squatted on a back burner, and she wondered if it was full of soup. Just how many bowlfuls could be waiting in there? Did the priests always have hot soup? Every day? Did they eat it more than once a day?

Useless questions.

"Come now," he beckoned, tilting his head towards the door on the far side of the room. It wasn't a choice to follow, there were no other options. But the priest had been gentle, and he had fed her warm food. For that, she would crawl after him over the rough floor if he asked.

How little it cost to buy her fidelity.

They passed through another door, but the next hallway was a little wider than the first, with a long, worn carpet running down the middle. It was softer on her feet, warmer, in fact the air itself seemed to lack some of the chill of the rooms upstairs. Or maybe she was just drying off and filled with warm food for the first time since she'd awoken in Hell. Anything was possible in a world that made no sense.

He stopped at a door just before a bend in the hall and knocked softly. "You may enter," a man's voice replied, and the priest led her inside. White curtains hung from the ceilings, cordoning off six small spaces in the room. Like an old hospital.

Had she ever been in a hospital?

There was no memory roused by the sight, but the man that stood from behind his desk made her stomach twist around the digesting soup. It was easy to see cruelty once you knew what it looked like, once you'd experienced it, and this man was cruel. Even if he was dressed like one of the priests, sans the white collar. Instead of the traditional marker, he had a white sash around his middle, keeping the narrower style of robe close to his waist.

"She is fresh from baptism," the man commented, approaching to run a finger down her damp arm, and she masked her shudder as a shiver.

"Yes. Her two hundred and sixteenth." The priest said the number in his quiet voice, but her heart stuttered in her chest.

Impossible.

She hadn't been in Eden long enough for that many punishments or calls to service to have happened. And the damage had to be serious for a baptism to be ordered, which made it impossible. She'd remember that many horrible things happening to her, even if she couldn't remember the good things, the things from before, she remembered everything in Hell… right?

Her stomach churned, nausea burning a path up her throat as she lifted her eyes to the kind priest to find him smiling.

Hell is empty and all the devils are here.

"She's still functioning," the man said, sounding almost impressed as he looked her up and down, but she didn't care about the cruel man. Couldn't listen to anything else he said.

There was no way. They had the wrong girl. The papers were wrong. She hadn't been in the baths that many times, she hadn't been here long enough for that. It had only been… *how long?* Time skittered away from her as she tried to think, as her heart raced in her chest and water dripped from her hair, running in chilling rivulets down her spine.

The priests were still talking, but she could barely hear them.

Words about God and grace and purity. All lies, but their voices were narrowing, growing softer, just like the lights. It was hard to breathe in the dim. Her heart beating too loud in the mounting quiet.

And then the world tilted and everything went black.

CHAPTER 4

A sharp pinch between her legs woke her with a jolt, and Danielle tried to shift… but couldn't. Body stiff, her eyes were sticky, refusing to open even as something hard and cold slid deeper inside her. Then there was another sharp stab of pain at her entrance coupled with a metallic *clink*.

"Ah, you're awake." It was the cruel priest, his voice light, but she felt his hand on the inside of her thigh as he pushed it wider and manipulated the thing buried inside her. "The sedative worked quite quickly on you. Have you been eating enough?"

Sedative?

Questions that she couldn't ask or answer through her stiff throat, and it took more effort than it should have to swallow. Her mouth was dry, like her eyes, but she finally managed to scrunch up her face enough to get her eyelids to open.

She was on a medical bed, surrounded by white curtains, her legs spread wide in stirrups. Strapped down at wrists, waist, shins, and ankles. The man at the end of the bed still wore no collar, and she wasn't even sure he was one of the priests, but he did lift his eyes to hers before another metal *clink* heralded a painful stretch inside her. A croak came from her throat, as close to a cry as she could manage, and he smiled.

"Hmm. You're a little thin, but I guess that is to be expected. And we should never question the decisions of the divine." He pulled a tray closer, metal clattering atop it before he bent between her legs once more.

Like a gynecologist.

A doctor. A word that she recognized, but like everything else she couldn't remember going to one. How much of her memory was missing? The woman had said she would remember almost everything eventually, but she seemed to be losing more. Two hundred and sixteen baptisms, here, in Eden — that couldn't be right. They had her confused with another of the women. Someone else. Not her.

Something stabbed inside her and a croaked cry escaped her lips as she jerked against the straps, tears leaking from her eyes when she squeezed them shut. Then there was another stab, another, and she tried to pull harder on the straps, but only managed to earn a sharp slap to her thigh.

"Be still," he commanded, though there was a gleeful edge to his tone that made her feel sick as the next stab felt too deep. Wrong.

Her inner muscles twitched as he withdrew a long needle from inside her, and then her cunt spasmed painfully hard around the metal still holding her channel wide. She whined low in her chest, unable to voice the horrible ache as her body cramped, seized. *What had he done?*

"There," the man said to himself, and then with another metallic *clink* the pressure was mercifully relieved as he slid the thing out of her to set it aside on the tray. Warm liquid seeped out of her, dripping down her ass, and she wondered if it was blood.

But why go to all of this effort just to kill her? There were so many easier ways.

His hands returned, pushing her legs wider until the stirrups seemed to catch and hold them farther apart. The position strained her hips, made the joints ache and her thighs burn, but there was no point in even trying to speak. Nothing she said would stop him. Eden had taught her that lesson well.

Swiping through the wet mess between her thighs, his thumbs slipped through her folds and spread her flesh wide apart. Then the man leaned close enough that she felt his exhale, listened to the slow inhale that sent a shiver over her skin. There was no gentleness to his touch as he pinched her labia, roughly massaging before pulling those tender lips apart again. Inside, her cunt was tensing, fluttering, twitching, but she closed her eyes to all of it. Tried to push away the strange sensations, the clinical way he inspected her, and the dull ache whenever he manipulated her flesh.

"Good, good," he muttered to himself when he finally stopped. Danielle opened her eyes to find him standing at the end of the bed. Tall, thin, almost gaunt. "Now, let's see how you perform in service."

No. She jerked against the straps, straining her voice to make some sound, to whine, but there was barely a grating sound as she forced air past her vocal cords. Toying with her folds, he stared down between her legs, and she braced herself for pain. She was used to the degradation of being a set of holes for men, but nothing prepared her for the agonizing stretch of just two of his fingers entering her. It hurt so much more than it should have. That horrible smile was back on his face as he worked them in, forced them deeper, bracing his other hand beside her hip so he could lean forward and watch her suffering. An almost silent cry was all that escaped as her lubricated cunt eased his entry, even as her body refused to open for him.

"Beautiful in your suffering. Like a proper virgin." There was a manic edge to the way he said the last word, and she shook her head, denying the word, but he only grinned wider as he pumped his fingers once more, driving them in hard before he finally withdrew. He chuckled low, eyes meeting hers. "Oh, I know that you're thinking of your calls to service, my child. But you have been baptized, purified by the Lord, our God. Made clean again so you can fulfill a higher purpose."

Shaking her head harder, she tried to whimper, to cry out as he plucked the white sash from around his waist and started on the buttons of his narrow robe. Jolting at the straps, she didn't even know why she was fighting. It was only making him happy.

It always makes them happy when you beg or fight or cry.

Swallowing, Danielle forced herself to stillness and stared at the ceiling, trying to remember every terrible thing that had happened to her inside Eden. The beatings where she'd been punched and slapped and kicked. Struck with batons and canes for disobedience. Whipped for punishment and entertainment. The vicious rapes in every hole she had. It had all been horrible, and for some unholy reason she had survived. She always awoke in the baptism baths. Clean and healed *through God's grace and love*, or so they said. Alive in this *haven* they had built for themselves, believing their monstrous acts to be blessed by Heaven.

But this was Hell.

The woman in the chain room had told her that, and she had been right about everything except for her memory. Danielle didn't even care about her memories anymore. She didn't harbor the hope of being saved anymore — there was just the wait for a death that never seemed to come.

"I am blessed to be the one to ensure you are prepared and, if necessary, I will provide any additional treatments you may need before your next baptism." He glided his fingers down her stomach, gentle until he pressed the heel of his hand into the softness above her pubic bone.

She flinched as he pushed down hard, like he was trying to crush her insides, but then there was another trickle of warm liquid leaving her cunt. Blood, or not, he swept his cock through it, prodding her entrance as he spread his fingers over her lower belly, fingernails digging into tender skin like a claw.

"Be joyful in your suffering, child. We all serve God in our own ways, and through suffering you may find absolution," he whispered reverently, eyes wide, manic smile spreading as he pushed in.

Muscles jerking, Danielle gasped as pain blinded her. It felt like he was tearing her, sawing his way inside with blades instead of flesh. She tried to twist her hips away but he held her in place. Pinned under his weight, captive by the straps, in ungodly agony as her core spasmed and cramped around the invasion. He forced another inch inside and groaned as her mouth opened in a silent scream.

"So good. So perfect." Licking his lips, he stared down at where their bodies linked. "Let's see how well you perform, my child."

It was useless to cry, but she did anyway. Tears slid into her hair, warm tracks on cool skin, and Danielle tore her eyes from him. Staring at the ceiling, she tried to escape like she had on so many other calls to service. There was no pleasure here, just a rending pain as he worked his way inside her. Whatever he'd done had made her cunt tighter than naturally possible, reducing everything to agony for his bliss. Nothing more than a body that he'd twisted for his own purposes. Grunting, he shunted another inch inside, and her voice croaked as she tried to beg him to stop.

"You can take it. You were chosen, so I know you can. You were meant for this." The man slid his hand lower to brush his thumb over her clit. "Remember, God honors those who serve."

He applied pressure to that bundle of nerves, rubbing her in merciless circles that made her tremble. It shouldn't have felt good, there should have been no way that pleasure could leak in around the edges of the agony. But it was there, torturous and horrible. Building like a sudden tidal wave, and then — an explosion of bliss. It was the inverse of everything happening inside her as something like an instant orgasm flooded wetness between her thighs. Everything blanked for a moment, empty ecstasy shutting down her brain, and she wanted to hold onto it… but it slipped away as quickly as it had come.

Desperate for air, for respite, drowning in a chemical overload that she couldn't even voice Danielle pulled at the straps. In the haze, he'd forced the last of his cock inside and her body zinged back and forth between the extremes of bliss and torment until she was shivering, taut muscles straining at her bindings. Angled above her, he watched it all with eyes too wide, his fanatical expression taunting her with a zealot's glee.

"See? The agony and the ecstasy. God often gives with both hands," he grunted through harsh breaths. "But we must accept his tests as well as we do his gifts."

Danielle shook her head, hair sticking to her cheeks as he began a relentless pattern. Hips pulling back and slamming forward, mercilessly fucking her until the bed clattered against the wall and the pain had her lungs seizing. Every thrust felt like being torn open, her inner walls cramping as her body tried to curl inward but couldn't. Just when she thought she'd finally black out, escape the nightmare, his thumb would return to her clit. Forcing her to come in a soul-jarring snap of obliterating ecstasy.

Minutes or hours could have passed in that hellscape, listening to his harried prayers, his fucked-up comments between grunts and groans, until he finally pulled out of her. Fist wrapped around his ruddy shaft, he jerked his cock faster and faster, one hand braced beside her waist as he bit down on a moan and spilled his seed in ropes across her stomach.

Panting, he slowed his strokes and groaned. Letting the last weak spurts pool at her belly button. "You are blessed, child," he whispered.

Danielle looked away, kept her tear-blurred gaze glued to the ceiling, tracing the tiny cracks that made the pale ceiling imperfect. If only they would spread, widen, bring the whole of Eden crashing down on her… maybe then she'd find peace. But if God existed, he wasn't looking at this place. Definitely not looking down at her, at the naked body that couldn't stop shaking. There would be no miracles here, no mercies, no freedom from this hell.

When the man appeared beside her again, he was already put back together. Clothed and smiling like the world was as good as the priests described it.

"This is the first of many blessings," he said. Tugging his sleeve up, he held it in place with one hand so he could smear the ejaculate across her skin without tainting his robes. Priest or not, it didn't matter. There was no one holy within the walls of Eden, and the nightmare had to end at some point.

Maybe they'd finally kill her.

"Drink this, my child. It will help you rest until they're ready for you." He wiped his hand on a small towel and then lifted the back of her head in a mockery of care as he held a cup to her lips.

Hollowed out, all she could do was stare as she obeyed and swallowed. It tasted like water, maybe a little sweet, and some of it spilled past her lips to the rough sheet beneath her, but there was no chastisement in his expression. Just that plastic smile carving out creases around his mouth.

As he walked back to the tray, he leaned between her legs and prodded the tender flesh he'd violated before grinning wider. "Only a little blood, very good. Still… another dose would be wise."

Returning her gaze to the ceiling, she clenched her teeth together and tried to block out the rest of his idle chatter and the sound of the metal tray shifting. None of it mattered. She didn't matter.

If there really was a God, he'd call her home.

CHAPTER 5

She had been dozing, lost in a place between waking and dreaming where she could almost smell warm food cooking. A perfect place where kind words hovered just out of earshot, and all she wanted with every tattered piece of her soul was to stay there — but in Hell that was more than she could ask for.

A pinch to her arm sent lightning through her veins, like a full body shock that had her heart pounding and ripped her back to reality. Danielle sat straight up, gasping and clutching her chest to try and make the traitorous organ still. Why couldn't she just die? Why did her heart continue to beat when there was no more will to live?

The kind priest grabbed her shoulder gently. "You must be calm, my child. Lay back down, the medicine is still working to wake you. Let it work, and it will keep you strong."

Turning away from his touch, Danielle frantically searched the space around her and realized she was in a normal hospital bed. There were no stirrups, no metal tray of horrors, and when she raised her wrists she saw they weren't even marked. A thin, gray blanket lay over her, and she threw it back to find the same was true of her legs. No bruises, not even a lingering redness, but she could still feel the tender ache inside with each strange, involuntary flutter of her inner walls.

"Pl—" she tried to plead with the priest, but her voice gave out, cracking into nothing more than an exhale of breath.

"She will have trouble speaking for a bit longer, but the cardinals are aware of that. It's a side effect." The bastard that had done all of this to her stood in a gap in the white curtains, smiling directly at her. Just as fervent in his joy as he had been when he was inside her.

Cardinals? Who are the cardinals?

Swallowing, she looked into the soft brown eyes of the priest, trying to make him understand what the man had done, but he couldn't see. Couldn't understand, or didn't want to. He turned away from her silent plea and shook the monster's hand. "I will remind the cardinals if they ask. They want me to bring her soon. How long until she can walk?"

Panic seized her chest as a terrible feeling swirled in her stomach. Something worse than death was closing in, she knew it, and the gentle priest was going to lead her to it.

The road to hell is paved with good intentions.

"No, ple—" Danielle grabbed onto the priest's robe as her voice broke, trying to make him understand, to make him see, but he ripped his sleeve away and stared aghast at her actions. She pressed her palms together to beg, or pray. Whatever he wanted if only he would stop it.

He answered her with a slap, not anywhere near as hard as the others that had chastised her, but it still stung and shattered whatever meek flare of hope had been born at his presence. She didn't bother touching the mark on her cheek. Bowing her head, Danielle clasped her hands together in her lap, hard enough that the tendons stood out in stark relief. Still, he *tsk'd*. "It would be a terrible disappointment if I had to take you to the chain room for your behavior instead of bringing you to the cardinals. The punishment would be severe."

It was a threat, a reminder to behave that she hadn't needed in so long, but for once that dank room filled with old chains and manacles didn't sound like a bad alternative. Whatever waited for her with the cardinals would be worse — and at least she knew the horrors that came after the chains.

"Nonsense. She doesn't need to go to the chain room, she's been very obedient. It's likely just the excitement of being woken up so rapidly." The man turned to her, still wearing that sick smile. "She is blessed."

The priest turned to scrutinize her, his soft brown eyes moving over her face as if he wanted to read her soul, or whatever was left of it. After a moment, he spoke in the gentle tone she'd come to expect from him. "What do you want, my child?"

A pointless question. A question he didn't even want an answer for… not *really*. The gentle priest was no different from the others. No, there was no good left here. Maybe there was no one good left anywhere, and this was truly Hell. A place where there was no salvation, no grace, no God. Swallowing, her throat felt a little less stiff, but her voice remained quiet and scratchy as she forced out the only answer they wanted to hear from her. "To serve."

"Good." The priest smiled, and it looked warm and genuine even though it was a lie. "We all make mistakes, child, and God forgives us in his limitless grace and love."

As ill as it made her, Danielle nodded.

CHAPTER 6

The walls were damp as they descended another set of stairs, although these were stone and seemed to take longer with their tight coil. Escorted in front and behind, with the gentle priest leading and the cruel one following, Danielle wondered if she slipped on the next damp step if the tumble would break her neck. The ache between her thighs was unrelenting, a consistent throb that reminded her of what the man had done, of what still felt so wrong inside her. It could all end if she fell. Just a slight lean forward, an angle of her foot. It was tempting, and she even tested the slickness of a stair, but then she saw firelight reflecting off the walls.

Then there were no more stairs to tumble down. Her chance lost.

Two men in large black cloaks, faces obscured by the hoods, waited at the bottom between twin torches. Beyond the reach of the flickering firelight was darkness, and if there had ever been a gateway to damnation — this had to be it.

"I was told to bring this woman to the cardinals," the gentle priest said, but as he stepped forward one of the men raised his hand, stopping him.

The other pointed at her, and then turned his flat palm to the ceiling and beckoned her forward with a single bend of his fingers. She was frozen, something beyond fear snaking down her spine and gripping tight.

"They will take her the rest of the way, father." It was the cruel priest, and she felt his warm hand in the small of her back as he nudged her forward.

Danielle moved robotically, taking small steps towards the dark figures, and when she risked a glance at the gentle priest he was still staring into the darkness as if he longed to walk into it.

Insane, they're all insane.

As soon as she was close enough to the men, they each grabbed their torch and began to move down the hall that looked to be carved directly from the rock. Large crosses, outlined in shining gold thread, decorated the backs of their cloaks. A robe she had never seen inside Eden, and she wondered if these large men were priests as well, or something else. Something worse.

"Remember, my child, God honors those who serve," the gentle priest said before he turned and followed the other up the stairs. Danielle stayed where she was, torn between the urge to follow him up the stairs — damn the consequences — or do as she was told and pray that it earned her some form of leniency. Some respite from the pain that she knew waited for her in the black.

The growing brightness on the walls around her made her

turn, and sure enough one of the cloaked figures was returning to fetch her. Bowing her head, she clasped her hands in front and walked to meet him. When he didn't begin walking again, she was sure he would strike her, punish her for the disobedience, but the void inside the hood only stared for a moment longer before he turned away.

This time, Danielle followed. A little slower than their long strides, but she was close enough to see them use a key to open the thick wooden door at the end. The hum of voices coming from within pulled her forward, the brighter light teasing her curiosity until she stepped through the doorway and into a massive room.

Black walls at least three stories tall towered above her, with beautiful pilasters carved directly from the stone. Ornate details in the walls and ceiling were highlighted by the flickering firelight from an immense fireplace at one end of the room. Even from so far away, she could feel the heat, and her feet turned towards it on instinct. Now the cloaked men were following her as she approached the long, oval table where men sat drinking and eating. A round of laughter rolled over them, and then they slowly fell quiet as one by one they turned to watch her approach.

Delicious scents hit her nose, strange for a moment until she placed them. Cooked meat and fresh bread. Saliva pooled in her mouth, her stomach rumbling, all fear replaced by raw hunger.

"Are you hungry, my child?" The first man to stand from the table was hard to see with the glare of firelight behind him, but he spoke like a priest. She wanted to nod, to say yes, to beg for the food.

But nothing is free in this place.

Meals were only earned through service. Mistakes and failures were punished with pain and hunger. There was no other way inside Eden, and for food like this she would have submitted without hesitation… but her body was wrong. The cruel priest had done something horrible, and no matter how much she wanted to remember the taste of bread — it wouldn't be worth it, even if she managed to keep it down after they were done.

"Come here." Another of the men spoke, turning in his seat to beckon her forward, but her feet wouldn't carry her closer. They were all dressed in rich red fabrics, more vibrant than she'd ever seen outside her hazy memories.

The cardinals.

Her core clenched, a dull cramp that awakened the lingering ache and made her press her thighs together. As several more cardinals stood, she swallowed the saliva in her mouth and took a step back.

"Bring her," a voice commanded. It was the cardinal at the far end of the table, the one sitting in a large chair with a high back. Like a throne, it caught the firelight with glints of gold in places. His command had silenced the others, and it was the two cloaked men who followed his order.

Each arm caught in a vice-like grip, there was no fighting their strength as they hauled her forward, half-lifting her from the ground when she stumbled. They dumped her at the feet of the cardinal, knees bruising on the stone floor as she stared at his crimson slippers. Not thick boots like the men she was called to serve, or plain black shoes like the priests, but scarlet, soft-looking slippers.

"My child, you are here to fulfill a great service to God. What do you say?"

It was a line from the priests' scripts, but she had no doubt this was where those words had come from. These men who ate luxuriously in fine clothes, hidden underneath the hell they had built. Long, frail fingers touched under her chin, lifting her eyes to his. A faded green in a much older face, creased by time, although he looked healthier than anyone else in these walls.

"What do you say?" he repeated.

"Tha—" Her weak voice cracked, and she swallowed. "Thank you, God." It wasn't much better, still scratchy and the fact that her voice broke on the last word felt appropriate.

The cardinal smiled, but it didn't reach his eyes. "Yes, we must always thank God for his grace and his love. Without it, we would all be lost. Without it, Eden would not exist as the last place for salvation. Here, my child, drink to ease your thirst."

A shining goblet was offered, filled with a red liquid to match the man's robes. *Wine*. Another flickering memory, like a picture in a book, only now it was in her hands. Bowing her head, she whispered the correct prayer of thanks, almost inaudible, but she hoped it was enough to get to keep it. To taste it. When she lifted it to her lips, she waited for someone to stop her, but they just watched as she tipped it up and drank.

"So pious, she prays before she drinks."

"The divine has chosen well."

"We are blessed for God to have sent her to us."

Danielle ignored their voices even as they came closer, drinking until she'd emptied the goblet. Soft laughter came from a few of them as she bowed her head and held it up where the cardinal could take it back.

"Here, my child. Have mine." Another large glass was offered, less ornate, but she dipped her head and began to drink it as well. Before she was done, the cardinal took it back. "Oh, not too much. It is watered wine, but in a delicate flower like you... moderation is best."

"Taste this instead." A hand studded with two large golden rings moved into her vision, a shining piece of meat held in pinched fingers. The smell of it had her leaning forward to accept it, open-mouthed as the grease and salt touched her tongue. Danielle closed her eyes and moaned low, greedily sucking his fingers for just one more taste. It was a hundred times better than the warm soup. A complete kaleidoscope of flavor.

The next offered her warm, soft bread, another something small and dark that was incredibly sweet. On her knees beside the cardinal's throne, she let them feed her like an animal. Licking fingers, sucking them into her mouth, unabashed as they rubbed over her tongue and her belly gradually became full for the first time since she'd awoken in Eden.

"That's enough. We don't want to make her sick on so much of God's bounty." The head cardinal ran his thin fingers through her hair, plucking at the knots.

Danielle almost whined but nodded instead. "Thank you, father," she replied softly, surprised to hear her voice without the strain.

"You sound much better, my child." Patting her cheek, he smiled and touched her shoulder. "Stand so the council may see you fully."

There was a tingling warmth spreading out from her belly that ebbed the fear she'd felt when their eyes had first landed on her and, as she stood, she peeked at them through her hair. This time their smiles seemed less dangerous, but nothing good lasted long in Eden.

"Here in our sanctuary you have been shielded from the horrors of the world, my child," the cardinal said, but he was looking across the table at the others as he told what must have been a joke.

Did the man have any idea what happened to women upstairs?

"Our enemies are wicked, evil men that have given themselves over to the Devil in their hunger for power. It is why Eden must be protected through whatever means God provides, for Eden is the last chance for salvation. We are the last line of defense in the holy war to ensure God wins dominion over the earth." The speech was made in a strong voice, echoing off the ceiling as his words rang down the long room, and beneath her feet Danielle could have sworn she felt the floor rumble.

Sounds of agreement came from each of the cardinals, many saying *'Amen'* as they made the sign of the cross. When their gazes returned to her, she bowed her head and clasped her hands, faking prayer as she avoided the stares and tried to forget the hunger she'd seen in their eyes.

"This evening, God has provided us with Danielle. A fitting name, my child." The head cardinal clapped his hands twice, and a string of men in the same dark cloaks as before walked out from the shadows on the edges of the room. Platters and plates were cleared away, leaving only the large containers of wine and the cardinals' goblets.

"Thank you, father," she whispered, eyes tracking the dishes.

Turning in place, she watched the men disappear with the food, mourning the loss as a smaller table was carried out. Round, it seemed to be made of stone, and was heavy enough that it took six of the cloaked men to place it between the long table and the fireplace.

"Do you know what your name means?" the cardinal asked.

"No, father."

"I will tell you." Another warm smile that didn't meet his eyes, even as he stood and extended his hand to her. She stared at it for a moment, wary. No priest had ever offered her his hand, and this was a cardinal. *The* cardinal, which meant that refusing it would be worse than whatever would happen when she laid her hand in his.

As soon as she did, he caught her hand in a grip much stronger than she expected, leading her around his throne to the round table. The gray stone had carvings in it, symbols and words she didn't recognize around the edge, and one large symbol carved in the center. It looked ancient, worn smooth by time, where even the edges of the carvings had a slight slope to them.

"Danielle means *God is my judge*, and you have been judged, my child. Judged and chosen to be part of this world's salvation." The intense look in his eyes had her stepping back slightly, but his grip tightened painfully and she whimpered. "Do not be afraid. God honors those who serve him."

"Let us bless you, child." Another cardinal took her other arm, pulling her toward the table, and she shook her head.

"You must give your thanks with all of your *self*," said another from behind, and then there were multiple hands on her, pushing and pulling her until even when she tried to struggle, she was overpowered.

"Please..." she whispered to the towering ceiling as they held her down to the stone. The heat of the fire was glorious on her skin, but it couldn't reach the hollow cold settling in her belly.

Everything in Eden comes with a price.

CHAPTER 7

Three of the cloaked men arrived with manacles and chains, and most of the cardinals stepped back to allow them to move her. One of them shackled her arms above her head, and the other two did the same to her ankles, running the chains through points beneath the table that bent her knees and kept her thighs spread painfully wide. When they were finished adjusting the lengths, her ass rested at the very lip of the table, and there was no give, no way out, no escape.

"Don't cry, my child. This is a blessing. So few are ever chosen to receive this second baptism, and the holy blessings we give you will protect your body and soul." The head cardinal trailed his gaze down to settle between her thighs where she felt her core clench tighter. "It is why you had to be purified, made new. Only the pure can be blessed."

"I'm not—"

"Shh, child. God has chosen you." One of the cardinals laid

his fingers over her lips, and when she tried to explain again, about the calls to service and the cruel priest, he moved his whole hand over her mouth and held it there firmly.

"Let us pray," the head cardinal said, laying his palms on her thighs as he stepped closer to the table. "God, give us the strength to baptize this woman of Eden. To mark her as one protected by the house of the Lord, and to cloak her in the power of the holy."

What could he possibly want to protect her from?

What could be worse than what she knew they would do to her?

The cardinal lifted his hands from her thighs, looking out at the others. "Fathers, I remind all of us that God shall never give us more temptation than we can handle, for in this we must serve him well."

"Amen," they chorused around her, and then two of the black cloaked men stepped forward to remove the elaborate crimson robe from the head cardinal. She couldn't see him well with her head pinned to the table, but once his skin was bared she could hear the sound of his hand working his cock and the low groan in his chest. Another cardinal pressed his hand into her lower belly, and she whined.

The lightest brush of her clit summoned liquid heat, and someone dragged their finger through her folds, spreading the wetness. She could only hope it made some difference to what the other bastard had done to her in his fucked-up version of a hospital.

"Give your pain to God," the head cardinal said as he lined up and then thrust in hard, tearing into her with one vicious spike of agony. Her scream was muffled by the hand over her lips, body pinned to the stone beneath her as the man pulled back and thrust again. Just as horrible, she wailed, finally able to voice the torment as her entrance was forced open and her inner walls seized and cramped. "Yesss..."—he groaned—"your purity, your suffering, is what will make the blessing strong, my child."

'*Bullshit!*' she wanted to scream. There was no purity left in her, not after every violent, debased thing that had been done to her inside Eden. She'd been fucked in every way imaginable, used and defiled, and it didn't matter that their baptisms healed her skin — nothing could heal the damage inside. The shattered pieces of the person she had been before their 'sanctuary.' Before this nightmare.

Hell. She was in Hell, and no prayer from their lips or hers would stop this torture or save any of them. God wasn't watching. God, if he had ever existed, was dead.

"Yes, my child..." The head cardinal started to thrust more quickly, the pain a vibrant, horrifying pulse between her thighs as he slammed into her again and again. Grunting and praying in stilted words as she cried uselessly. Finally, he pulled free and she felt the first warm drops of his seed land on her belly just before someone stroked her clit in quick circles and she arched off the stone as the orgasm possessed her.

A blinding wave of pleasure that obliterated the pain for a glorious flash. A perfect moment of bliss that in a less broken person might have been a religious experience. Her moans bordered on screams as she shook, and through the haze she heard the head cardinal speaking.

"See how her body accepts the blessing? How God turns her

pain to ecstasy in celebration? She has been chosen and will deliver us our weapon. Remember, each drop of her blood spilled through her service proves her purity, and we must do our part. Now, continue and baptize her, cardinals."

His last command was barely complete before another cardinal was between her thighs, ignoring her whimpers as he forced his cock inside. A fresh wave of pain that made her scream, and the very room seemed to shake in response, but no one else reacted. Sobbing, she strained at the manacles holding her arms taut, and then another pair of hands pressed her forearms into the stone to prevent it. It was too much. She was raw and torn, but he kept fucking her.

After an endless amount of pain, he pulled out and spilled his seed, and just like before she was granted an orgasm. A carnal lie that told her nerves to expect more pleasure even as she tried to fight against it, but it was impossible as the bliss drowned her. Lost in the bone-melting haze, she slowly became aware of hands stroking the still warm ejaculate over her belly, her breasts, and then another cardinal ripped his way inside her.

Merciless, they seemed to only thrust harder when she screamed, cried, wept — not even pausing when a roar hurt her ears. But maybe the thunderous sound was only in her head.

Maybe she was losing her mind.

Four, five, six of them and she was somehow still conscious. The pain was unavoidable. Even as her muscles grew weak from the constant strain, even as she prayed to God to let her die, the torment that felt like knives tearing at her never wavered. She wailed in agony, begged and pleaded, until even her voice started to give out. Their seed was spread across all of her exposed skin, fingers dipping into her mouth to feed it to her once she was too weak to fight back at all.

She'd lost count completely when the pain finally began to ebb, when every thrust didn't feel like pure torture, but there were still two more unholy men who used her until they too were spent. Each forced orgasm still rocked her, leaving her weaker each time, but finally... they were done.

Would they leave her alone? Let her sleep? Finally kill her?

"Cardinals, our blessed Danielle has been baptized by this holy council. Through her suffering she shall have absolution. Through her purity our weapon will be forged." The head cardinal was nearby again, but she didn't bother opening her eyes even when he blocked the warmth of the fire with his body. "We thank you for your gift, my child."

"Thank you," the others solemnly repeated.

"God has made her strong, and made her body ready for the final baptism." Those words got her eyes to open, and she whimpered as she looked up at the cardinal's red robes, glowing with the light of the fire behind him. A dark, damned figure.

"The Devil," she whispered, knowing the evil in him first hand, but he looked down at her with a strange look on his face.

"No, child, you are protected. He cannot harm you, and with your body you will bring us a weapon to win this war." Raising his hands, he clapped once and the cloaked men returned. Dazed, she almost smiled when one of the men handed the head cardinal a knife.

Finally, death.

"Cardinals, we know that under the law almost everything is purified with blood, and so our last gift is the final baptism. It will protect her purity, just as her blood has purified her acts of service."

The cloaked man that had provided the knife pushed the hood back from his face, revealing a shaved head, and pale skin. As the cloak was pulled away by others, he moved between her legs in silence. Young and muscular and naked, he leaned over her, arms braced by her waist, and she shook her head, tensing as she prepared for him to violate her.

"My child, we thank you for your sacrifice and your service to God," the head cardinal said.

Then he dragged the knife across the man's throat. There was a terrible choking sound, wet and sucking, as hot blood poured over her stomach and chest. Cloaked figures caught him by the arms, holding him as he bled over her and died. It was the head cardinal who laid a hand on the man's forehead to lift it, letting the last drops spill before he dipped his thumb into the mess on her stomach and traced a cross on her forehead. Almost exactly where the gentle priest had.

In shock, Danielle shuddered, wanting to scrape the man's blood off her skin, and when her tongue moved to wet her lips, she tasted copper.

They had killed him. *Murdered*. Broken a commandment under the guise of a holy rite. If she had not been hollow already, she would have mocked their hypocrisy as he was dragged away by the others as if nothing horrible had happened.

Damned. We are all damned.

Broken, she didn't fight as the cloaked men returned and undid her chains. They had to lift her from the stone, holding her upright when her legs wouldn't support her while blood flowed over her skin, dripping down her thighs.

"Remember that you are thrice blessed and protected by God, our Lord. No evil will have dominion over you, my child, even as you give all of your *self*." The head cardinal gestured and the cloaked men half-carried, half-dragged her after him as the cardinal led the way to the other end of the massive room. She didn't walk. Couldn't. She let her feet scrape the stone, limp in the grip of the cloaked men. Watching the blood dripping off her to leave a bloody, crimson trail that the other cardinals followed.

This time, the roar that shook the floor beneath them was definitely real. Everyone paused for a moment, and Danielle raised her eyes to the door just as a rumbling growl emanated from behind it.

"What..." It was the only word she could say before smoke wafted in front of her face. Choking on it, she ended up breathing more of it in as she coughed. Sugary sweet, her head was spinning a second later, but they kept her face close to the golden object. Suspended on a chain, it swayed, spilling forth gray smoke that clogged her lungs. Suddenly dizzy, she would have collapsed completely without the men holding her up.

"Danielle, your faith will keep you strong even in the presence of evil. We all serve God in our own ways, and you alone can use the gifts God has given woman to herald our victory." The head cardinal opened the door himself, and she was dragged forward until the pitch black of the space beyond was inches from her toes. Confused, unable to make sense of his words, she struggled to lift her eyes to the darkness. "Give God your pain, child. He honors those who serve him," he whispered.

A searing pain suddenly sliced across her shoulders, and she cried out just before she was shoved forward into the dark.

CHAPTER 8

The heavy sound of the door locking behind her was nothing compared to the low rumbling growl that seemed to come from everywhere. On scuffed hands and knees, she tried to find the source in the darkness, but there was nothing to see. Worse, the terrible pain in her back confirmed that the head cardinal had used the knife to slice her open.

"Why!" she weakly yelled at the door, or at least she thought it was the direction of the door. She felt the anger burning somewhere underneath the pain, a dull rage that ate at her, and she had to bite her cheek to stop the tears. They had taken everything from her, brutalized her over and over, and for what? To shove her in a cell so she could die as slowly as possible?

Maybe that's why they fed me. So I'd last longer.

A harsh, hysterical laugh burst past her lips, and she tried to sit upright, but the skin on her back pulled and she hissed air through her teeth. Another growl buzzed through the dark, just to her left, and she pushed herself away from it despite the pain. Too weak to run from whatever it was, she wiped at her running nose and scrubbed the tears and blood from her cheeks. "Please don't hurt me anymore. Just kill me. End it, please."

"Hurt you…" a low, strange voice echoed, this time coming from the right.

Danielle reached out, sweeping her arm through empty space even as the wound on her back spilled more blood. It hurt, but she'd been in pain for so long that her body just felt tired as she sagged and sat back. Head spinning, she wanted to lie down and be done with it. Let death come, let the growling thing eat her, and move on to whatever came next.

Heaven, Hell, a black abyss of nothing.

She'd take her chances.

"So broken," the thing purred just behind her, and even though her body tensed, she didn't move.

"Just kill me," she repeated, and something like a laugh, but not, echoed in the darkness from all sides. It was disorienting, and she realized as her skin buzzed that the pain was fading a little. There was a humming in her blood, like a song, and the beat of it thrummed along her nerves.

Maybe this is what dying feels like, the brain shutting down.

It's nice.

"Death is not so nice." The voice was in front of her now, and her eyes played tricks, creating a hulking shape out of the darkness. A shadow darker than the black, but when she reached for it her hand passed through empty air and wiped the illusion away.

"Death would be a gift," she replied to the nothingness.

"So many other things to do…" A faster reply, almost against her ear, and Danielle turned as she felt her hair move. Like a light draft in the stagnant space. "I can show you."

"Do whatever you want, just kill me when you're done." Sighing, she cursed herself internally for speaking to whatever delusion the smoke, or her failing body, had created.

"You are not dying, nor delusional, Danielle." The voice was close again, just behind her, and the way it said her name made her skin break out in shivers. "Hmm… do whatever I want? You would give yourself to me?" it asked in a low, purring thrum that ran down her spine.

"Does my answer matter?"

"Of courssssee…" Once more the voice was everywhere, scattered and echoing, and she shifted, trying to find a comfortable position, but one did not exist on the rough stone floor. "Will you?"

Sighing, Danielle looked up at where the ceiling would be if she could see. She had looked up at the ceiling during so many terrible things inside Eden, wondering if God could see her suffering, wondering if it would ever end — and there had never been an answer. There was not going to suddenly be one in the dark after being brutalized by the cruel priest and then the cardinals. This weak attempt at hope was just some last-ditch survival instinct of her brain, and she was done with that. Done and ready for the end. "I just want to die so I can escape all of this."

"I can take your pain away." The low, soft voice was like a whisper directly in her ear. "I can make you feel better, feel pleasure, feel powerful."

Closing her eyes, she tried to block it out, instead focusing on the memory of a warm voice reading from a book and the silken feel of her sister's hair as she'd braided it. She remembered the café table, the playful smile of a young man that may have been someone she loved. In her head she saw flashes of trees swaying in the wind, rain falling on a pool creating thousands of ripples that she could never count.

The presence was close, almost like a buzz against her back. "I can help you remember," it purred.

Turning her head, she could have sworn she saw a shadow move, and she swallowed past the dry sweetness in her mouth leftover from the smoke. "How?"

"You are so broken… I can put you back together, Danielle." A breeze against her face, warm, like something big had exhaled. "I can give back what they took from you."

"What are you?" she whispered, and heard the thing's soft, echoing laugh.

"I am trapped. Just like you."

"That's not what I asked," she muttered, a frisson of unease coiling around her spine as she waited for pain… but none came. It had been so long since she had dared to speak her mind that it felt good to argue, to contradict, and no one slapped her or hit her for doing it.

"I want to hear all of the words you want to say," it purred close by. "I want to hear all the noises you make."

"Tell me what you are."

This time the breeze came from behind, warmth blowing over her neck. "Your priests call me a demon."

"Are you?" she whispered, a twist in her belly that could have been fear beneath the haze of the smoke.

"What I am they cannot comprehend, but others trapped me here a long time ago. They want my power, use what little they have stolen to heal their people." Another purr, still behind her, and it made her ribs buzz. "But I can do so much more for you... you just have to say the words."

"What words?" Her voice shook a little as she asked, because if the cardinals were right then this would be true damnation — but what was the alternative? To die in pain? Or the chance that *maybe* they drag her out of the darkness, put her in the baptism baths, and return her to service?

She'd die first.

"I cannot damn you, Danielle." Warmth coated her back, but there was nothing touching her, just... warmth. It soothed her as a soft rumble shook the room. "Just give yourself to me."

"You'll help me remember?" she asked, picturing sunlight on green grass.

"Yessss..." The voice scattered, echoed, and then moved around her as it continued. "I will fix what they have broken... as long as you give yourself to me."

"Okay."

"You must say it, Danielle." The voice was close, like a whisper against her ear.

There was nothing left. Nothing of herself to protect, no scrap of her soul worth saving. Even if the thing lied, even if it meant death and damnation, at least it would end. She licked her lips, swallowing before she finally said, "I give myself to you."

The rumble grew, louder and louder until the floor shook underneath her, and then she felt something wet move across the cut on her back. Like a big tongue, it stung for only a second, but before she could even wince the pain was gone. "Good," the voice hummed, still low, but stronger. More powerful. "You taste wonderful."

Turning, she realized the fresh wound was completely healed. Not a tug on her skin, or an ache. "That's amaz—" Danielle gasped and let out a short scream as she was suddenly lifted into the air, completely off the ground, and she flailed, scrambling to grab onto anything in the empty black.

"I am here." A low chuckle that turned into something closer to a growl as huge hands landed on her hips. Then she felt warm breath between her thighs, and she tried to snap them closed but found she couldn't. "You bled here," it said just before the tongue swiped through her folds.

"Oh my—" Shivers took over as the large tongue stroked and slid, teasing her clit with each long sweep, and when it dipped inside Danielle's eyes rolled back. The flicking motion inside her was too much, and she suddenly came with a stunned cry. Legs shaking, body shuddering, there was a buzzing moan against her cunt as it returned to long licks. "What a-are you doing?" she asked.

"Fixing what they broke." Another lick that teased her and sent her into little aftershocks. "You were perfect. They just could not see it."

"I wasn't a virgin," she tried to explain, waiting for the thing's attitude to turn violent, but instead she heard more low laughter.

"That does not matter to me." The hands left her floating in the dark, bereft of touch or direction until the voice came from the empty air above her. "It means nothing at all. And you were not a virgin when you were taken."

"Taken?" she asked, reaching her hand up to find it, but there was nothing there.

"Like all of those here." The voice moved, disorienting her. "You can remember."

Something reached in, tapping like a piercing headache behind her eyes, and then she saw flashes. *Rubble near a collapsed wall. Her home. Her father putting her and her younger sister in the basement. The shouts, the gunfire, her sister crying quietly on the floor as Danielle picked up a baseball bat. The door opened at the top of the stairs, but it wasn't her father. She screamed for her sister to run, watching as the man put his gun away while he swaggered down the stairs, unafraid. Danielle shouted, swung the bat, but he caught it, ripping it free of her hands before he hit her with his fist. Pain bloomed across her cheek as she fell, hitting the ground hard. From the floor she saw her sister scrambling up the shelves, out the window, but there was someone there and Mary screamed.*

"STOP!" she shouted, almost screaming it, and the memory cut off with a sudden dizziness as the dark took over. The vivid afterburn of the scene still blazing inside her mind. It had felt so real, like she was standing there. Feeling it, smelling the smoke. Her cheek almost seemed to ache, but she touched it and realized it didn't. It had been real, once, but not now. It hadn't happened now. Tears in her eyes, Danielle tried to sit up while floating in air and found it impossible. Listing in the void, her chest ached with the pain of fresh loss that was long past. Then, like a flick of a light, she remembered her father's name. Isaac. "What happened t-to him? To Mary?"

"I can only show you what you once knew, what they took from you. I do not know everything, Danielle." A soft purr from underneath, and then she felt warm, hard muscle behind her as large arms wrapped around her. "Perhaps their holy crusade was not the best memory to return at first. How about this?"

Another piercing headache and then she felt the cold. *Sitting in snow, tying the laces on skates as Heather and Landra shouted at her to join them. Clumsy steps onto the ice and then she was flying, with cold air whipping her hair, chapping her lips, but it didn't matter because everything was perfect. The sun was bright, glistening off the ice on the trees, and her best friends were racing her across the pond.*

"Ice skating... interesting." The rumble in the thing's chest faded as it released her from the vision and exhaled against her hair. "A much better memory."

"Yes, th-thank you for that." Swallowing, Danielle wiped her eyes and tried to turn, but the thing wouldn't let her. It had power, *real* power, and that was almost more terrifying than its hold on her. Tracing her hands over the arm wrapped across her body, she tried to understand what it was, but all she could tell was that the dimensions were wrong. Strange. Too large compared to her to be any kind of human. "You're... exactly how big are you?"

"I am as small as I can make myself and still have substance." Another low laugh. "This memory is good."

Before she could tell the thing to wait, to give her a moment *to breathe, she was tossed into it. Someone was kissing her, softly, with a hand on the side of her neck. On a bed in the afternoon sun, a handsome boy leaned up and grinned down at her as she felt his fingers glide down her body. Teasing a breast, lightly pinching her nipple until his mouth replaced it, sucking it in as she parted her thighs so he could slip his fingers inside. Somewhat clumsy, but there was so much excitement, their hearts racing, breath coming too fast as she moaned, and he kissed her to keep her quiet. 'Now?' he asked, and she nodded, a blush heating her cheeks, and then he moved between her legs. Kissing, easing in slowly, gently, asking, 'Are you okay?' between kisses until their bodies met, fitting perfectly. No pain, just fumbling, new pleasure. 'I love you,' he whispered, like he always did, with a kiss to her nose and then her lips. 'I love you too,' she answered, and it was true and good as he moved inside her.*

The vision, memory, whatever, ended just as abruptly as it had begun, leaving her with a tingling in her skin that had the ghost of a smile spreading across her face. She was still able to feel his lips on hers. Christopher's lips. A slightly younger version of the man from the café, which meant they had stayed together. Her first love, her first time with a man had been good. The thought made her happy and sad — bittersweet. To know she'd had love, but it was already gone.

"There are more of those memories." One large hand moved between her thighs, and she gasped as one thick digit slid inside without any pain. "More, where he is better. I can show you them while I touch you."

Shaking her head, she tried to close her thighs, but her legs wouldn't move any closer together. "I want to know everything. Everything they took."

"I can keep the bad memories away, give you your childhood, your Christopher, your—"

"No!" Grabbing at the thing's huge hand, she tried to pull it away, but there was no moving it. "Stop, please… I just want to know my life. You said you would give back my memories, give back what they took."

"And you gave yourself to me in exchange." A low rumble as a second finger tried to work in beside the first — too big. Whimpering, she was about to argue when it spoke. "If you want to know more, here."

"Wait!" she shouted, but it was too late. A thump behind her eyes and *she was on her knees. Hands bound with chain to a pole behind her back. There were more women to her right and left, but too far away to be of help to each other — and talking to each other always earned punishment. The man in front of her had his pants open, his dick in hand as he approached and grabbed her hair. 'Open up,' he demanded, and when she clenched her jaw, he backhanded her, and pain burst in vibrant white across her cheek. Ears ringing, ripped upright, but this time he shoved in, instantly choking her. 'Hit me with your teeth and I'll take them out.' So many more men like him. One after another. Her lips felt bruised, split, throat aching as another told her to 'Open' and she did without argument. His cock went too deep, too fast, forced into her throat and her stomach heaved. She threw up, but it was nothing more than water and seed, because that was all she'd had… but the man hit her anyway, kicked her before someone else pulled him back. Left her bound on the floor. Bleeding and crying, praying to God for help.*

Ripped back to reality, Danielle could only sob, jerking in the tight grip across her ribs as she tried to escape the men from her memories. Free of them now, but she was still trapped in the darkness, aching as her body strained to accept the creature's fingers, feeling the thick digits moving in and out as the memory made her throat ache in sympathy. She wanted to scream, but she bit her tongue instead of yelling and cursing at the thing like it deserved. It could hurt her easily. With more memories, with its strong, too-large hands and arms, and she knew she was still just as powerless as she had been chained to the pole. Licking her dry lips, she whispered, "I… didn't remember them doing that."

"I know," it rumbled low. "It was from shortly after you were taken."

"How long ago?" she asked, gasping when its fingers pushed deep again, straining the limit of how far her cunt could stretch. Clenching her teeth, she stifled the whine, holding her breath until it finally eased them back. She had a new threshold for pain after the cardinals, but her body still had limits.

"Hmm…" The creature's other hand slid to her breast, and she couldn't help but clench around the fingers buried deep when it pinched her nipple, tweaking it just like Christopher had. "Time is confusing. Perhaps four or five years ago."

Danielle's heart stuttered, her head swimming. "That's impossible."

"It is true. You just do not have the memories." A low rumble as those fingers rocked in and out, the wetness easing their path, her body somehow adjusting to it. It purred against her back, a soft rumble like distant thunder. "There are no good memories from this place to give you back."

That was easy to believe. Eden was Hell, but part of her still wanted them, wanted the truth, just to know what had happened. What had been done to her body, to her, but she didn't say it aloud. "Why can't I remember?" she whispered.

"You are human. Your body was never meant to be healed like that, Danielle. Each time you were injured, they put you in the water, but it has been too many times, and the water cannot heal your mind. Just your body. So frail and mortal... you have been damaged so often, so *easily*." As if to make the point, the thing spread its fingers inside her until the painful stretch had her whining and clawing at its hand desperately. A hot exhale brushed over her hair and down her front as it returned to simply thrusting them. "It is not surprising your mind is broken."

"But they said Go—"

The thing growled, arm tightening until her ribs creaked. "What they call their *baptism baths* is a power stolen from *me*."

"Stolen?" Twisting her head, she tried again to look at the thing, but there was only the hint of some kind of shadow in the black as its fingers stayed still inside her. "How?"

"The water. The runes the humans used to bind me here, to imprison me, seems to lock my power in as well. I cannot reach past these walls, but my time here has resulted in some of my power leaching into the water." A low, rumbling chuckle buzzed against her back. "I believe they discovered the effect on humans by accident... after they tried to drown me with their water supply. Now they give credit to their god for what they have stolen from *me*."

"It was all a lie," she whispered. She'd known it, she felt she'd always known it was a lie. That the priests, all of Eden was just a corrupt hellhole.

"It is, and you are correct. You never believed them. Such a smart girl, Danielle." A gentle touch turned her face, but her eyes closed before she could see anything in the dark. Unable to open them, she felt its mouth on hers. So much larger, but it tasted sweet as its tongue teased hers softly. Pleasure pulsed, and a moan slipped from her as she rocked her hips against those delving fingers — until a third tried to fit.

"No, st—" Cut off with another kiss, face held firm by one strong hand, she whimpered as the thing forced her legs wide, bending them towards her chest. In the new position it was able to work the third in a little bit, steadily stretching her as she tried to plead for the thing to stop. Her begging broken by each flick of its tongue past her lips.

"You gave yourself to me, Danielle. I will not be patient much longer. Open for me." The thick fingers pushed harder, and she cried out, tears springing to her eyes as the creature's hold on her became complete for a moment. In empty air, she was left floating while it moved around her in the black. Suspended in the nothing until the thing's tongue slid over her clit and three painfully thick digits thrust at her bruised cunt, trying to stretch her even further.

Pleasure competed with pain, mindlessly terrifying, unable to move. Just as an orgasm was about to crest through the torment, she regained some control and screamed, "STOP!"

"You would rather not feel pleasure?" it asked, a feral growl under the words, and then she fell. A short scream escaping before she hit the ground hard.

Danielle had no idea how far she'd fallen, only that her shoulder hurt, and she'd hit her head. More pain. Just more pain. Had the priests known it would do this? That it would want inside her just like them? What had they thought fucking her would do? What did they think their twisted drug would do other than make everything hurt worse?

Sniffling on the floor, she rolled to her side slowly, wishing that her body would finally just give up, that her heart would stop beating before worse could happen. Her head pounded as she pushed herself up with a weak whimper. "You— you said you wouldn't hurt me," she accused in a soft voice, staring up into the black, and the only response for a minute was low, echoing laughter.

"I never promised that. I promised to fix what they had broken, to return your memories in exchange for you. *That* was our pact, and yet... you fight me. Even as I seek to offer pleasure, you make demands." Another rumble that shook the ground as she swallowed the lingering taste of charred candy from its kiss. "If you want your memories, Danielle, you can have them."

Something snapped behind her eyes, like the pop of a rubber band, and then there was only suffering. A surge of pure agony as she screamed. *Screaming, always screaming. 'They like it when you scream.' A rough hand grabbed her, bent her over the side of a bed a second before the man shoved his cock in her ass. So much pain. Another flash, and she realized she was hanging by her wrists, in thick cuffs, but one wrist was already broken, and the baton was still in his hand as seed leaked down her thighs. 'Piñata time,' he laughed before he swung and broke a rib. Then the world shifted, and a man loomed over her... shouting, yelling, and she curled up on the floor. Unable to remember what she did as he kicked, punched her. Face down, a different time, a different man lifting her ass into the air, spanking her just before he started to fuck her as she sobbed. Bleeding. A man on top of her, inside her, thrusting so hard her cunt hurt — but then it was someone new — again — again. Her throat, her pussy, her ass, a hundred, two hundred, three hundred, there was no counting. Some hit her, hurt her on purpose, some just used her for the warm body she was. The flickers slowed, and she sat down on the floor of a hallway where a girl lay dead. Bloody, the shape of her skull was wrong. The priest touched her hair, ordering her to pray. Shivering, she woke up in the baptism baths. Over and over and over and over. Sometimes the men wanted her to serve them before she went to the priest. Before the priest fucked her on the floor, another on her knees, another taking her throat. Then there was someone whipping her, she couldn't see them, but she wanted to die. She wants to die. She just wants to die.*

"NO!" Tear-streaked, Danielle screamed and gulped air in the pitch black. Sobbing hysterically, trying to fill lungs through broken ribs that were not broken anymore. Confused. Nothing felt right as she scratched nails over stone, on hands and knees, screaming whenever she had the breath to let one tear from her throat. There was so much wrong, though not wrong anymore, but her mind could still remember the burns on her hands that taught her not to steal food. Everything seemed to be happening at once, and also be over, and eventually there was nothing to do but cry and scream as the memories tried to sort in her head. All of it worse, so much worse, because people had done it. Just people. Humans.

"Yesss," the voice answered, smug and self-satisfied as the horror slowly forced her into silence. "You really do it all to yourselves. This place was not my idea."

"I can't," she whispered, too afraid to live with what could happen — what had already happened. "Please... I want to die."

"No, there is no chance of that." The thing lifted her from the ground, spreading her thighs painfully wide to fit between them. Purring, it kissed her, all burned sugar sweetness with the tip of its large tongue moving between her lips. "You are mine, you gave yourself to me"—a trail of kisses down her throat as it continued—"you are never going to die, Danielle. I can fix you, just like I said. Mentally and physically. If I hurt you, and that is unavoidable, I can heal it. Sometimes you will accept me, and sometimes I will take what I want from you. But you are mine and I *will* have you."

"Please just kill me," she begged, whimpering as the thing lifted her higher and its massive cock pressed against her entrance. "No, no, stop! Please!"

"I can fix it," it purred. A sharp pull at her hips and the head popped in, a searing ache as her cunt stretched. When she tried to put her leg down to push away, they were suddenly back in the air, floating as it forced another inch or two in and she screamed.

"Don't hurt me anymore," she cried, begging as the pain spiked and ebbed.

"This feels good, Danielle… Be with me this first time, feel it all." It growled low, arms wrapped tight behind her back as it thrust deeper. Something tore and she screamed, hiccupping on a sob as pain shot like lightning up her spine. "Yessss… let me in. Feel me inside you. I will hear all of your sounds eventually."

"Please," she whimpered as it thrust deeper, and the agony stretched with her. It groaned against her, a dull vibration as it held her tight to its massive body.

"So tight, so warm. This was meant to be." Its tongue invaded her mouth as she cried out, overwhelming as it took control and its cock throbbed inside her. "Mmm… you are mine. Perhaps in time you will even bear a child like they had planned. Although it would never serve them. It would be *ours*."

"No..." Shaking her head, she felt something deep inside shudder. Confused and lost in the pain as it lifted her a bit and then pulled her down by her hips again. Her sob of pain was echoed by its satisfied groan.

I will never bring a child into this hell.

"You would be glorious swollen with child, filled with my seed." It purred and traced sharp nails down her spine. "It could even make you stronger. There are so many possibilities for us."

"Why?" she whimpered as it moved a little deeper inside her. "Why a child?"

"A child might let me escape." Sliding her up and down its shaft, she shuddered, choked on a sob as with each downward thrust a little more made it inside. "I have never bred a human before, but we have all the time we need to see if it is possible, Danielle."

"Please... no..." Crying, she found her arms trapped behind her back, unable to move them as it controlled every inch, every movement.

"If you play nice, I can give you pleasure with the pain."

Desperate, she nodded, and tried to relax enough to let the thing's massive shaft inside her. Pleasure bloomed out from where they were joined until the pain was manageable, as if it took nothing for it to erase the ache inside her. Just as it had been nothing to show her the memories, both wonderful and horrible. Thinking of the torrent of memories still trying to find a place in her head, she shuddered. "Was— was it all just a lie? Everything?"

"What your *priests* told you?" The irritation in the thing's voice was clear.

"All of it. God, the Devil, Heaven, Hell… is any of it real or was it all a lie?" she asked, voice shaky, and then she cried out as it rolled them so she was on her back, once again on the stone floor. Knees bent high as it slid another few inches in successfully. For a moment, there was just her scream of pain as her body shook, straining to adjust.

"Shhh," it hushed her with a purr, ecstasy pulsing from the agonizing place it was trying to split her. Confusing, like two different versions of her body overlapping. One tortured, one pleasured.

Her breath shuddered. "Pl-please, just tell me."

"Heaven and Hell?" The thing laughed, a low and disturbing sound directly by her ear, and she couldn't stop the tears. "And what would I be in that dichotomy? Your devil?"

Maybe.

It didn't need to be said aloud, the thing could read her mind. Knew her better than she knew herself. As it started to fuck her, still not all the way inside, she hovered between bliss and torment and knew that the thing could control all of it. Every sensation, every memory, everything. It was choosing for her to suffer right now, just like it had chosen to dump the most horrific memories into her mind at once — and this was only the beginning. Still trapped in Eden, still doomed to suffer, to remember or forget on a whim.

Danielle would have to beg for the good memories, would have to *play nice* and ask it to take the memories of Eden back. She wanted to forget ever being baptized in Eden.

There could be a different memory for how she ended up

here, something new, because whether it existed or not... this was Hell.

And she was trapped with a monster.

She was damned.

EPILOGUE

LATER

"It is almost time, Danielle…" The voice echoed around the room, not anchored to any specific point, but she just kept her eyes closed and ignored it. Soaking in the pool, she felt good. Relaxed. It didn't really matter that she knew the water was cold, that some part of herself could still feel it, because she could *also* feel warm water wrapped around her like the pool was some sort of luxurious bath — and she chose to focus on that version of reality. Still, it was strange to be aware of both.

But everything in her life was strange.

Like the darkness inside the thing's prison. She knew it was dark in the stone room, that there was no light… and yet, now she could see the dull gray of the darkness and then the pitch black of *it*.

Opening her eyes, she turned to where she could sense it

moving. A scattered, shapeless shadow passing across the massive space. She knew it sensed her too, sensed her looking at it — or it read her thoughts — any of it was possible. It was capable of anything. It did horrible things and miraculous things. Completely unpredictable. Insane. Perhaps it had lost its mind long before she'd ever been thrown inside its prison, and one day it might lose enough of it to finally kill her.

To set her free.

One moment the creature was nothing more than a blurry shadow, and then it had form. Legs, arms, a massive body, and the thing was walking toward her. She could hear it, the heavy steps on the stone, but that meant nothing. It could be soundless when it wanted to. Everything about it was fabricated for her. For her *limited perception.*

"Are you comfortable?" it asked, standing so tall above her that its head seemed to blend into the ultimate black high above them.

"Yes," she answered aloud even though she didn't have to… but she preferred it. It was unnerving to have a conversation using just her thoughts when the thing always had to speak for her to understand. Of course, sometimes thoughts were all it allowed her. Those times when it took her voice away so that she didn't distract it from the *true things* in her mind. Usually it wanted to hear the noises she made, the moans and the screams, but lately it had been silencing her more and more often. Whenever it wanted to know if she understood, if she believed it.

Not that it likely helped. She didn't even know if she believed it.

The things it said to her, whispered in her ear, were madness.

"I am not mad, Danielle," it said, answering her thoughts because she hadn't said any of it aloud. A low sound like a chuckle came out of it, and then it stepped closer. "Do you still doubt me? Even after all I have shown you?"

"Does it matter?" she asked, because she knew it didn't. In this hell it had never mattered what she wanted or didn't want, it had never mattered if she said *no*. Not to the ones in her visions, and not to this… whatever it was.

"Soon you will see that I have not lied to you. That I have never lied to you," it rumbled, crouching beside her to lay one of its large hands over her breast, squeezing. She felt the rush of artificial pleasure that it used as just one more method to control her. It never got any easier to suddenly have her clit pounding, her cunt squeezing around nothing as she arched into its touch, body on automatic. A different kind of violation as it manipulated her mind, made her feel what it wanted her to.

It pulled away and the pleasure cut off instantly, leaving her panting in the water, clenching her teeth against the urge to beg. *That* was probably what it wanted right now, and she refused. It had everything else. It had everything it wanted from her, and it would never end. She'd tried to play its game in the beginning, to acquiesce to every demand, terrified of the pain and the visions it could shove inside her head — but it always hurt her anyway. Had taken memories away only to give them back. Had forced itself inside her with no gift of pleasure just to hear her screaming, sobbing, pleading. So, she had given up on trying at all. She refused to be *joyful in her suffering*.

Now, she merely existed. Breathed. Drank the water. And, even though she always fought it as long as possible, she swallowed mouthfuls of its seed when she was hungry.

Although, her body wasn't hungry as often anymore. Not tired. Not thirsty.

Perhaps it was finally killing her.

"You are doing very well, Danielle," it said, an edge of humor to its tone.

She rolled her head back, looking straight up at the dark outline of its form, but she didn't bother to speak. It could sense her doubt, her bitter hatred of it and everything else.

"Come here," it beckoned, and she rose out of the water because it willed it so. Floating above the surface as drips ran in rivulets over her skin. The sensation was still odd, still felt like it should be impossible, but her entire world was insane. This impossibility was just one more piece of it. Just like the creature that owned her inside and out.

Wrapping large hands around her shoulders, it pulled her closer and let her drop slowly until her feet touched the stone. "What were you thinking about?"

"Death," she answered honestly, but it only chuckled as it released her.

"As I have told you many times, you need not worry about death. You are mine, so you are safe." It moved backwards slightly, the edges of it blurring.

"Not safe from you," she mumbled.

Another scattered chuckle, like more than one voice was mocking her until the sounds coalesced into one heavy word. "No."

"What do you want?" she asked, and it reached forward to touch her cheek before palming the entire side of her head.

"Danielle... did you forget again?" There was a soft edge to its voice, and she felt the odd flicker behind her eyes that she connected to it digging through her mind. "Do you remember where you are?"

"In your prison," she answered, turning her face away from its touch to try and end the invasion of her mind, but it just turned painful. Her knees buckled with the sharp stab between her eyes, unable to even feel the ache of her knees impacting the stone as she grabbed onto the sides of her head. Whining, begging with incoherent pleas for it to stop.

Suddenly, the blinding pain disappeared, and she sagged forward, hands planted on the ground as she gulped air, tears painting warm tracks down her cheeks.

"You are fighting me, Danielle." It crouched beside her, still so much taller as it forced her to sit back on her heels so it could brush one large hand over her hair. "You know better than to fight me."

"I'm not doing anything," she whispered, staring up at the empty black shadow that made up its face. Featureless, even though she could feel lips when it kissed her.

"I am not sure whether I find it promising, or troubling, that you are doing it without trying." It petted her again, brushing over her hair several times before resting its palm at the back of her skull. "Can you sense the changes within you?"

"I don't know."

A buzzing *hmm* floated around her and then it squeezed the back of her neck. "That was honest. Your mind still has its limitations, Danielle, but those will fade in time. You will see."

"I can see *you*." Swallowing, she tried to identify a nose, eyes, *anything* inside the dark shape of its head, but there was nothing else. Just its shape. "Almost," she added.

"That is good, Danielle. You will know this face soon enough, but now we must discuss the plan again." It shook her gently. "That means you need to focus. Remember."

"Just tell me what you want," she replied softly, not wanting it angry. She didn't want any more pain, she just wanted to get back in the cold, but warm, water again.

"I want you to tell me where you are, where this prison is."

"It's..." she started to answer but trailed off as she searched her memory and found a hole. A space where that information used to be, almost like she could picture the outline of the missing knowledge. It scared her, and she felt her breathing pick up as tears stung her eyes, not wanting to answer because it would mean pain.

"I will help you." The thing lifted her into the air, floating high above the ground, with only its hand against the back of her skull. "This will hurt, Danielle."

"No!" she shouted, desperate to avoid it, but the piercing headache came back almost instantly. Like someone stabbed a needle through the center of her forehead and then held it there, twisting it as vicious flashes forced themselves into her awareness. *Men holding her down, inside her. Slapping her, hitting her. Wrists in chains as someone forced their cock past her lips, into her throat so there was no air. No way to breathe until she finally gasped awake in a cold bath, bound to a submerged table, where more men told her she was lucky. Baptized. And then the priests. The Church. The cardinals. The prison. Eden. Eden.* Eden.

"Shhh." It tried to calm her as she snapped back to reality with a choked sob, a scream that wouldn't stop until it placed its warmth at her back and wrapped its arms around her, squeezing until her ribs ached.

"It— this is…" The words wouldn't leave her lips as she tried to twist out of the thing's grip, but it wouldn't let go, wouldn't stop *shushing* her like some errant child. There was more floating in her head, visions that were actually memories — memories she didn't want. So much worse than the flashes it had last given when it wanted her to scream, because there were so many more. Like hulking beasts waiting at the edges of her thoughts, just waiting for her to turn away so they could take her down. "Take them back," she demanded.

"No."

"Take it back!" she screamed, rage filling her as she tried to shove its impossibly strong arms away from her, but it simply adjusted to pin her arms to her sides. Held to its hard chest, helpless, crying pathetically as a whole new wave of hate crested inside her. "Why?" she growled.

"Because you need to remember. I have taken the memories away before, but you will need them." It shushed her again as she screamed, trying to stop the subconscious horror reel unraveling in her mind. They had done so many things to her, erased them with baptism baths, baths created by the power from the thing holding her tight. "Danielle, do you remember where you are?"

"Eden," she spat. The word made her sick to her stomach, made the rage burn at the back of her throat, fists clenched as she remembered her last moments in the light with the cardinals. Remembered the cruel priest and the endless litany of horrors from the men who visited their *sanctuary*.

"Good," it replied, its tone still so calm. "Now stop fighting it, stop trying to forget."

She ignored the thing, trying to remember how empty and peaceful she had felt in the water. She wanted that back. The barren wasteland her mind had been for a short while, but as she pushed the memories away the pain returned. That same sharp stab behind her eyes that made her cry out, dissolving into tears as she squirmed against the monster trying to ruin her.

"Stop fighting me and it will not hurt."

"You don't know what… you just don't—"

"I see it all, Danielle, and I want you to remember what they have done to you." Another sharp twinge between her eyes buckled her resolve, left her limp against its hard form as she was forced to relive a thousand terrible things, a thousand nightmares. "Shh, that is all done. You are above that now."

"Why won't you just let me die?" she whispered, and that strange laugh echoed around her.

"Because I need you." It relaxed its hold on her and she pulled in a deeper breath as its face brushed the top of her head. "And you are finally strong enough."

"I'm not strong."

"You are, it is just one more thing you have ignored." One of its hands drifted over her skin, claws dragging in thin lines until the claws disappeared. "I have changed you, but they began this process long before I ever touched you. They put me inside you, my power. Bathed you in it over and over and over."

"So?"

"And you survived, Danielle." Its hand slipped between her thighs, and she flinched, muscles twitching even though she knew she couldn't close them. "You survived me as well. Having me inside you."

"I don't want to survive." She shook her head as it delved one thick finger inside. "I want you to end this. No more, please."

"I cannot do that, Danielle." It started to move back and forth, slowly teasing at the wetness her body responded with as the pleasure returned. A rush like heat washing up the front of her, landing like a scalding blush in her cheeks before it wrapped around her. It was disorienting but compared to the nightmares lurking in her mind she didn't care.

"What are you?" she asked, still so lost, so helpless under its control. So uselessly human when compared to the thing that wasn't a demon as the priests thought — but something else. A question that she knew she had asked so many times before. She could remember each of them. "Please, just tell me what you are."

"Does it matter?" it asked in return, pushing in a second and then a third finger alongside the first, but she could handle it now even though the stretch made her whimper.

"Please, just tell me," she begged, biting down on a whine as it spread her legs, bending her knees without actually touching her. Folding her into the position it needed to work all three fingers deeper. She couldn't stop the pathetic cry as the first twinge of pain between her thighs made her spine stiffen. "Please…"

"There are things that existed before your kind. Things that you have no word for, things you cannot comprehend so you never named them. That is what I am, Danielle."

"That doesn't mean anything," she whined, cunt already twitching around the invasion.

"It is the only answer. I have already told you that I am not some simple demon." It hummed against her ear, tongue tracing up her throat as it worked to stretch her until the strain of its fingers bordered on bearable again. "There is no word for me, no concept that you would understand, Danielle. At least, not yet."

"When?" she whispered, moaning as another flood of pleasure overwhelmed the next stretching thrust. Suddenly on the edge of an orgasm that scattered her thoughts for a moment.

"If you can ever see past this world, you might understand, Danielle. But first, you must get out of this prison." It turned her head, brushing its lips across hers. "You have to get out of here to discover what you are capable of."

"I don't understand," she whimpered, tilting her hips as she sought the obliterating pleasure the thing could give her when it wanted to.

"You have to break the seal. Set us both free." Its tongue flicked past her lips, tasting her for a moment. "Then you will have your vengeance."

"I don't know if I can…" Flashes passed behind her eyes, things it had forced in, things not hers. The mad things. The things she had locked away with Eden in the darkest places of her mind, but it had set them free again and she could feel the last pieces of her sanity fraying as the images wouldn't stop.

"I know, Danielle. Shhh, let me give you something good before it is time."

Time? There was no time, not here, and she wanted to remind it of that, of the terrifying things it had shown her, but before she could speak... everything was gone.

There was only sunlight, a warm, soft bed at her back — and Christopher. Brown hair, bright blue eyes, twin dimples as he smiled down at her. 'You are so beautiful,' he whispered before he kissed her. Tongue dancing with hers as she clung to him, pulled him closer, so desperate to feel him against her. To keep him there.

'Please don't leave me,' she begged, voice betraying the unending sadness in her chest, but he simply laughed and kissed her again as he settled between her thighs.

'Why would I leave you? I love you,' he replied just before he caught her lips again. A soft moan buzzed against her mouth, turning into a playful growl as she lifted her hips so she could feel him rubbing against her. 'Want me?' he asked, grinning.

'Yes.' She nodded, hands at his back to pull him closer. 'Please, Christopher?'

'I am always here, babe.' He shifted, bending one of her knees gently before he lined up and pushed against her. There was a brief flash of pain, but he kissed her to catch the whine as it escaped, not letting up as his hips thrust in shallow, insistent dips. 'You can take it. You can take all of me.'

'It hurts...' She gasped as he thrust harder and forced himself inside, agony rocking her until a sudden rush of pleasure overwhelmed it. Her head spun, dizzy as he groaned above her.

'Yessss, Danielle.' He kissed her again, sealing his lips to hers, and then another thrust brought more pain.

'AH! Wait, Christopher, please?' Whimpering, she looked between them and saw where they were joined. He wasn't all the way inside

her, but he looked like he always did. It shouldn't have hurt, shouldn't feel so painful.

'I know what you need,' he purred, kissing her mouth, her jaw, her neck. Reaching between them he started to rub that little bundle of nerves. Small, sweeping circles that made her feel warm and tingling as pleasure rushed through her veins. Her muscles relaxed, legs spreading wider for him to ease deeper. 'There, all better.'

'Just go slow?' she begged, lifting to capture his lips again as he moved within her, more hurt that washed away with the next pulse of bliss. There was an ache deep inside, like he went too deep somehow, but she forgot it as an orgasm crested and wiped out everything but pure ecstasy. She cried out against his lips, holding onto him as she felt his arms wrap around her. Another brilliant spike of pain in the haze, and then his hips were pressed to her, and she felt the rumble of his moan.

'You are perfect, so perfect...' His tongue tangled with hers, pleasure rebounding inside her as he started to thrust steadily, creating a delirious friction that had her arching and asking for more as the pain abated and another orgasm took her breath away. Completely filled, every nerve ending alight with ecstasy, body warm and hungry for more. Christopher began to thrust harder, and she was able to take it, riding the flood of endorphins in her veins so that even the brief flashes of pain were nothing but passing thoughts. 'I knew you could do it,' he whispered.

'I love you,' she cried out, another delirious crash of pleasure overtaking her as he thrust hard and came deep inside her. She could feel the warm pulses of his seed filling her, moaning with him as his weight pressed her into the bed and the ache between her thighs became a buzz at the back of her brain.

'I love you too,' Christopher panted, kissing her as he eased from her slowly so he could lie by her side. 'Danielle?'

'Yeah?' She smiled sleepily as she turned to look at him.

'If you loved me, why did you let them take you?' There were no more dimples in his cheeks. Instead, he looked upset, brows pulled together as he looked at her.

She shook her head. *'I didn't let them, Christopher, I—'*

'Why did you let them take you away from me? From your dad? From Mary?' He frowned, reaching out to touch her arm. *'What happened to Mary?'*

Panic clutched at her lungs as she held onto his arm. *'I don't know, but I'm here now. I'm here and—'*

'Do you think they did the same thing to Mary? Do you think everything that happened to you… happened to Mary too?'

'Why are you saying this?' she asked, fighting back the tears. She tried to sit up, to cover her ears, but Christopher grabbed her shoulders and pushed her back to the bed.

Leaning over her, she couldn't do anything but stare into his wide blue eyes. *'They took you away from me. They took Mary. Just like they took our moms, just like they took everyone. The Church took you away from me.'*

Memories broke inside her, remembering the day the sky burned. The panic she'd felt the day her mother hadn't come home from work. The way Mary had kept asking where mom was, the way her father had made phone calls and paced. It was the last day her father had let them out of the house.

'Do you think they killed me like they killed your father?' Christopher shook her as she started to cry. *'Or do you think I joined them?'*

'No!' she shouted, but he just shook her harder.

'They took you away from me. Why would I have refused?'

'Please stop!' She wrapped her fingers around his arms, holding on tight as she pleaded. 'I don't want to talk about this. Please, can't you just hold me?'

'No. That is not possible, Danielle.'

'Why not?' she asked, sniffling.

His eyes were empty, his voice too quiet as he leaned closer. 'Because they took you.'

The bed disappeared behind her back, and she fell. Away from Christopher, away from warm sunlight and softness and gentle kisses, down into the dark where she collapsed on rough wood. A hard kick landed on her ribs, knocking her to the side as she coughed, whined.

'Stupid whore, this is all your fault.' Another hard kick to her stomach, and she retched, holding out a hand to stop him.

'Don't. Please don't...'

'They said you need to suffer, whore. That's the only way to end this insanity.' He reached down and grabbed a fistful of her hair, wrenching her upright. 'If you hadn't sinned, if all of you bitches hadn't sinned, none of this would have happened.'

'No!' she shouted, unable to understand how the asshole believed any of it, but he backhanded her hard.

'This is all your fault,' he growled and shoved her back to the floor, pushing her thighs apart as he climbed on top of her. Catching her hands when she tried to fight, he slammed them to the floor above her head and spit in her face. 'You have to learn your place, whore.'

'NO!' Danielle screamed just as he thrust inside her.

The rage burned the memory away, and she opened her eyes

to the dull gray darkness and realized she was still screaming. She remembered everything. Every good moment before the sky burned. Every horrible moment after. She remembered the insanity of The Church. Their broadcasts, their messages, their call for a return to 'The Laws.'

They had destroyed everything.

Her life, her family, her world. They had destroyed *her*.

"They tried to," the thing purred against her back as she felt gravity return, and it placed her on her feet. "But they failed to destroy you. Instead, they made you strong."

"That wasn't a memory," she growled. Nausea creeping up the back of her throat as she felt the *wrongness* of Christopher.

"Not at first, that was something... more."

"It was you," she accused, already knowing it was true before she even heard its rumbling chuckle. She could feel the ache it always left between her legs, and its seed was leaking down her thighs.

"Yes. I wanted to feel you again, and you prefer Christopher, do you not?" Smug satisfaction in its voice, and she clenched her teeth against the urge to rant and rave — it wouldn't make a difference.

"Why ruin it with the asshole at the end then?"

"Oh, your call to service? That was real. Your first." A soft *hmm* buzzed through the air between them. "Just a reminder. He was so righteous as he hurt you, simply because The Church told him that it would fix everything."

"Another lie," she spat. Barely able to contain the hatred she felt as she remembered her sister's screams, her own screams. "What do you want?"

"I only wish to give you the opportunity to destroy them, Danielle." It grabbed her wrist, pulling her arm forward until her fingers brushed metal. The door. "Call out to them. The men will come for you."

"And then?" she asked, head pounding as her heart raced. Remembering the cardinals in their crimson robes, the horrors they'd inflicted. All of it was because of The Church. The men who led it, the men who had hurt her. *So much pain.*

"Then you will set us free. Then you will have your vengeance." It released her wrist, brushing its fingers across her hair. "You will know what to do."

She felt its presence scatter behind her, the dull rumble of its power vibrating the door and the stone beneath her feet.

"*Ssssound ssscared,*" it whispered from the darkness, many voices echoing.

Running her hands along the door, she tried to find a handle, but there was none. Not in its prison. Slapping her palms against it, she shouted, "Let me out! Please!"

It wasn't hard to summon the tears, she could still remember Christopher's face from her real memories, his smile and his dimples. Could still see the panic on her father's face the last time she'd seen him alive, could feel the terror when she heard Mary scream.

She hit the door harder. "Please! Cardinals, please, help me!"

To her surprise, she heard the metallic scrape of a key in the lock, the tumble of the mechanism. A second later, light blinded her. Grabbing onto the frame of the door, she stumbled forward, hearing a man gasp and mutter a prayer. *One of the cardinals.* Cold hate washed through her, and she moved towards the sound, forcing her eyes open as they watered, revealing the blurry shape of the man in his red robes. She grabbed onto them, fisting the fabric to pull him closer.

"It is a miracle," he whispered, just before she grabbed him by the throat and squeezed.

"No. Not a miracle," she growled, feeling the fragile bones in his neck grind. His eyes were wide, panicked, and she knew he'd ignored the same expression on her face. The silent plea for mercy, for kindness, as he'd violated her along with the rest of them. With a twitch of her hand, she felt his neck snap. So brittle. So easy to give him the death she longed for.

The door.

Turning around, she saw the empty black of the doorway, and then looked at the stone around it. Intricate carvings by the hundreds, and on instinct she slammed her fist into one of them. It cracked as pain radiated up her arm, but then it was gone. The ache disappearing as she did it again and again. She could feel it inside her, its seed still leaking down her thighs as shouts rose behind her, and she struck the next block of carved symbols again. Knuckles bloody before the first man touched her, she recoiled instantly. Twisting, she struck him in the chest to knock him back, moving to the other side of the door to slam her sticky fist into the other side. More cracks spreading, thin sparks of light escaping as more stone splintered.

More.

A dull rumble shook the wall, fragments of stone falling as two of the robed men grabbed her and yanked her back.

Somehow, she pulled away, backhanding one, and she watched as the hood dropped away and a crimson arc flew from his mouth as he fell.

"Don't touch me!" she roared, and the floor rumbled beneath her feet.

"My child, be at peace. You have been blessed and—" One of the cardinals started to speak and she screamed to silence him.

Again. The door.

"Don't!" another of the cardinals shouted as she faced the doorway and brought her fist into the next section of unbroken stone, reveling in the gratifying way it buckled. Too old, it was brittle and ancient. That was why it spiderwebbed with cracks as she found the central carved piece at the top of the door and hit it even harder. The sound as the stone split in half was loud, echoing through the massive room with an earsplitting *snap*.

Then the floor was shaking, a localized earthquake that she held no fear of as the darkness bled out of the doorway and she stepped back, moving aside just in time for it to pour out like thick, oily smoke.

The cardinals screamed as it covered them, but Danielle just stared. Watching as sprays of blood flew through the air, accompanied by the strangely wet sound of snapping bones. It played out before her in slow motion. Gore and horror that didn't summon a single feeling of pity inside her. The smoke purred as the last body fell, and she felt its voice rumble out of the haze. *"Take your vengeance, Danielle. Destroy them all."*

"No. Leave the women alone," she whispered at the

towering cloud of black. "Please," she added, remembering that it could hurt her too if it wanted. "They've suffered enough."

"*As you wish*," it growled, and then it flowed fast. Almost swimming through the air until more of the black robed men came through a door in the wall. They were carrying swords, actual swords, like out of some old movie. It sped toward them, cutting through them with ease, bodies falling as it passed, leaving pools of ichor on the ground beside clattering steel — and then it was across the room just as fast. Shattering the door she'd first come through when they'd brought her to this hell.

That was the way out.

But… there were still cardinals here.

She could hear their prayers, their pleas for mercy to a God that had never listened to anyone inside Eden. Walking over the bodies in front of her, she moved slowly to the table where the fire still burned behind it. The stone table was gone, but the massive oval one was exactly where she remembered. Several of the cardinals were hiding beneath it, babbling, and she wondered if this was the first time they'd ever felt fear.

"My child! Danielle!" The head cardinal crawled from under the table, pulling himself up by his throne as he looked between her and the doorway it had gone through. "No matter what it whispered to you, you should not have released it, you—"

"Oh God," one of the cardinals whispered as he crawled from beneath the table with another. "She has been blessed."

"Silence!" The head cardinal snapped. "Danielle, you must

come with us, my child. We will protect you until it is safe. Until it leaves this sanctuary."

"No," she answered, and she knew it was the first time they'd actually listened to the word. They glanced at each other, and she felt the cold swirling inside her. All of the emptiness that craved their deaths, their suffering. Penance for the things they'd done. To her, to everyone. "What did you think would happen when you fed me to that monster?"

"It was God's will, you—"

She screamed, cutting him off as she stomped forward and grabbed him, dragging his frail body onto the table with a jerk of her arm. "Was it God's will for you to torture me? To hurt me over and over and over?"

"Only through suffering can women find absolution! The first of you ate of the tree, woman damned mankind. You sinned and dragged man down with you. It was God who chose your punishment. Your monthly pain, your pain in service, your pain while creating life, which before only He had the power to do. And so, yes, you have suffered. God gives with both hands, my child. But, now, you are chosen. To set this world free and—"

Suddenly, her hand was inside his chest, just under his ribs, and she felt the wet warmth, the flickering pulse of his heart as her fingers closed around it and ripped it free. For a moment he continued to blink, blood staining his lips as he stared up at her and watched her throw his heart into the fire. She growled, hoping he had enough awareness left to hear her. "I am not chosen, and I am *not* your salvation."

Turning away from the corpse on the table, she prowled around the end of it towards the cardinals frozen in fear.

"I'm not yours at all," she whispered, and they ran. It wasn't as difficult to catch them as she'd imagined. It was even easier to break them. But their screams did nothing to ease the emptiness inside, the cold quiet as she thought of Mary, Christopher, her father, her mother. Everyone alive in the flickers of memory that her mind was still trying to process.

Leaving the cardinals behind, she walked out of their secret space. Through the darkness and up the spiral stair. When she came to the carpeted hall, she saw the wine-colored stain of blood in a thick streak, followed it until it ended at the closed door of the hospital room. There was no strike of fear as she opened it, no moment of horror as she saw the mangled corpse of one of the priests on the floor. A fear-filled shout drew her attention to the cruel priest, another of her tormenters, only now he was bound naked to a bed in the middle of the room.

A gift.

She could sense the thing somewhere inside Eden, moving fast in a random pattern, and she was sure that the quiet whisper in the back of her mind was its voice. It didn't matter, all she cared about was that it didn't hurt when it whispered behind her eyes.

Low, gurgling shouts came from the cruel priest as he jerked against the straps. Panicked, trapped, vulnerable like she had been. Blood spilled from his mouth and she moved closer to see that his tongue was gone.

It almost made her smile.

"Do you think that you're beautiful in your suffering?" she asked, tilting her head as his fists clenched on the other side of the straps. "Do you think your God will forgive you for what you've done? *Absolve* you because of this pain?"

More incoherent noises from the man. And he *was* just a man without the robe. They all were. Wrapping her fingers around his limp dick, she stroked and watched as he shook his head.

"No? You don't want me to touch you? Hurt you?" Rage flooded her suddenly, the memory of the agony she'd experienced at his hands clenching her fist tight, and she heard him wail as flesh tore. But as she opened her fingers, all she could think of was how ecstatic he'd been to tear into her. To make her scream and sob. "You should be joyful in your suffering," she hissed, but all he did was scream as she tore his mangled flesh free.

Sneering, she wiped her hand off on the sheet, watching as his eyes rolled, limbs pulling at the straps like they would suddenly fail to hold him when they had held her down to a similar bed.

Slowly, his struggles waned, turning into quiet moans of pain, and that was when she turned away. Leaving him to bleed out, to suffer, as she walked out of the room. She could still hear his sobs of pain as she wandered the long hall, but not even those noises could bring her any kind of feeling. Danielle felt numb. Broken. Emptied out as she found her way back towards the wooden door where the gentler priest had fed her before he'd turned her over to be violated.

The door opened easily, revealing the simple room where Priests were huddled near the benches. In the quiet place where for so long they'd eaten warm soup and lied. She recognized their faces from flickering glimpses of memories she wanted to avoid, and as she stared, they begged, pleaded, promised that God would still forgive — until she broke the first bone. Then they only screamed, damned her, cursed her to an eternity in the pit of fire as they died. Danielle could remember being afraid of them, of their power, but they seemed so small now. Weak and small.

It was as she climbed the wood steps that she finally heard the chaos happening above. Feminine and masculine voices alike, all drowned in fear, but still muffled behind the doors. Danielle opened the first one off the narrow hall, passing into the stark room where priests pretended to make the violence okay. Pretended that it was grace, *love*, from a God that had abandoned all of them.

She wanted to burn it all down.

A thrumming rumble passed by the door, in the main hall, and she knew it was the creature. An old thing leaving blood in its wake, taking revenge for its captivity on the monsters that had taken a broken world and bent it to serve them.

Danielle stared into the small fireplace, wondering why she had never been brought to the room where a fire burned. Ready and waiting to dry her off, to ease the ache of the cold baptism baths. If they had wanted to pretend grace, they could have at least offered her that. She traced the backs of the chairs set up in a half-circle around the flames, soaking in the heat as her flesh turned pink.

What would it have cost them to offer such a small kindness?

They could have fucked her on the wood floor here just as easily as they could have in any of the other rooms. She could have gone to her knees and sucked the cock of whoever wanted it as she enjoyed the warmth. Without question, she *would* have, like she always had when they'd demanded it.

Another flicker of rage and she threw one of the chairs. It snapped against the wall, one of the legs breaking off, and she picked it up. Eyeing the fragile wood, the wooden planks beneath her feet, and then she stuck the end of the chair leg into the flames. Watched as the tip blackened, burned, and finally caught fire. A weak flame, but still... fire. A fitting way to destroy Hell.

"This is for your gentle touch, priest," she whispered, dragging the fire across the desk where papers sat askew. Hissing as they burned, as the flames hungrily spread, devouring the handwritten pages. The door banged open behind her, and she felt its presence. A heady buzzing in her head as she refused to look at it.

"*Come*," it commanded, and she did. Carrying her makeshift torch with her as she followed, watched it tear priests and other men to pieces as its shadowy mass engulfed them. She wanted the sight to bring her joy, relief, *something* — but there was just not enough left inside her.

All of the horrors, the memories, the time spent inside Eden and with *it* had hollowed her out.

Changed her.

She didn't feel human, even as she heard women scream, watched them run ahead of the thing that she didn't fear anymore, because inside the cold in her chest she couldn't feel anything. It led her outside, into the sunlight, and she stood there as women streamed past them. Occasionally, she would hear it growl, feel the rumble and the warm spray of blood against her backside.

There would be no survivors among the monsters who had built Eden. The only monster left would be the one that gently took the burning wood from her hand.

"What do you want, Danielle?" it asked, its voice more normal, less multifaceted.

"I want it to burn."

"As you wish." Glass shattered, and there was a whoosh of air behind her as it left her, but she kept her eyes forward. Outside for the first time since they'd ruined her life. Stolen everything. The horizon was almost empty, only fields of grass as far as she could see, marked by the fleeing shapes of other women. They continued to run past her as she walked across the courtyard. An open dirt space where a lone cat walked as if there wasn't destruction raining down less than a hundred feet away. A parking lot of dusty, abandoned vehicles filled one side in front of the building, but they were ugly to look at, so she turned away and focused on the freedom she was supposed to have — but didn't.

She could feel the thing moving through the massive building behind her, like they were tethered together. Connected. It made her eyes sting as she clenched her jaw and watched another too thin woman bolt past her. A short, stone wall bordered the front of the property, a long dirt road leading off into the distance, cut off by the slope of a hill to be picked up again at a different angle. With the hazy blue of the sky hanging above her… it made it all look too pretty, too perfect.

Danielle walked until she stood by the wall, able to trace her hands over it as she watched a small herd of deer leaping away from some of the running women.

"You took your vengeance." It said from behind her, and she heard the scratch of its crafted feet on the dirt as it made itself known.

"Yes," she replied, shrugging a shoulder. "Some of it."

"Do you want more? There are others. In other places." It moved closer to her side, and she smelled smoke, saw the dark cloud of it staining the sky as the wind carried it in front of her.

"I don't know."

"You have all the time you want to decide, Danielle." It stepped even closer, several feet taller than her with smooth, inky black skin. "I have access to all of my power now. There is no limit to what I will grant you for freeing me."

"I think…" *I want to die.* The thought floated, and she heard it chuckle low.

"No, Danielle. You will not do that," it replied, running its dark, clawed hand over her belly as Eden burned at their backs.

"Will you ever let me go?" she asked, turning to look at it, and it had been right. In the pitch black of what it had for skin, she could see shining dark eyes, a nose, lips. She could see it, but it didn't make whatever it was any better.

"No. You gave yourself to me, Danielle." Its other hand moved to stroke her cheek, the claws shrinking back into its fingertips before they touched her. "That pact cannot be broken."

"You could break it," she whispered, and it didn't answer. But it was true, she felt it, but she also knew it would never do it. "How long was I in there with you?"

It let out a soft sound as it brushed her cheek again. "There was no time at all when we were together."

Rage flickered, and she shoved its hands away from her. "How long?"

"Out here? Two days." It grasped her hips, turning her so she had to face it, and she tilted her head back to meet its eyes as it continued. "But what does it matter?"

"I guess it doesn't," she answered.

"I will make you happy, Danielle. Would you prefer me to look different?" Its shape blurred as it released her hips, and her eyes hurt so she had to close them to block out the sight of pitch-black skin morphing and fuzzing at the edges. When she finally opened them again... it was Christopher. A perfect copy, down to the dimple that punched into its cheek as a lopsided smile passed over its face. "Like this?"

"Don't," she growled, turning away from the lie.

"Then show me what you want, Danielle." It held the side of her face, and she felt that strange flutter in her mind. It was searching her memories, but there was no pain as it finally smiled with Christopher's face. "Ah."

Another blur that made her clench her eyes tight and turn away. "Stop. It doesn't matter."

"It does for now, Danielle. Until you can accept me as I truly am, I can create a form you will enjoy more." She heard nothing for a moment except the roar of the fire and the whisper of the wind, but then she felt it touch her shoulder. "Look."

Sighing, she opened her eyes and saw a handsome man in front of her. Dark hair that fell across his forehead, darker eyes, and she felt like she recognized him — but there was no memory connected to it. "Who?" she asked, and it smiled with its beautifully-crafted face.

"You do not have a name for him, but you have liked him." It moved closer, pulling her against the hard, muscular chest that was still completely out of proportion. Still too large to be a real man, but not as tall as its other form. It leaned down, brushing a kiss across her lips. "You have touched yourself to this one."

"No," she argued, turning away from the kiss, but it caught her face and she was frozen, muscles locked up as she was forced to accept as it tasted her lips, her mouth. No control over her limbs, even as her body shook with the effort to move.

"Do not fight me, Danielle. I do not want to hurt you. You have given me so much... My freedom"—it reached between them, running soft, human hands over the gentle round of her belly—"a child."

"Don't," she growled, trying to ignore it. Trying to forget that the cardinals had called it a blessing with wide eyes, as if they had any idea what their insanity had created. *She* had no idea what was growing inside her. What made her capable of breaking stone and bone with ease, what let her tear the flesh of the men who had hurt her.

"Imagine what you will be capable of by the time our child is born," it whispered against her lips, and she felt the iron-clad grip of its power ease back.

"Yes, imagine..." she replied, feeling bitter as she looked down at her blood-soaked arms and flexed her hands where the sticky texture of it mounded in the valleys between her fingers.

"You are already above them, Danielle. Already different, changed." It trailed kisses down her throat with its false face, continuing to trace gentle caresses over her stomach. "It is why you have accepted me more easily. It is why I could fill you. The child will be powerful on its own, but that power is already a part of you. I am a part of you, and always will be."

She wanted to die as she felt the rush of pleasure up her spine, the sudden surge of need as its hand dipped down between her thighs. "Please don't do this."

"Pleasure is one of the few benefits on this plane of existence, Danielle, and you cannot deny me." It lifted her in its human-looking arms, carrying her through the opening in the wall to the soft green grass on the other side.

Laying her down gently, it looked down at her with dark eyes, and she could see the echo of the real thing behind the mask. Still, this was more tolerable than the monster that had first stood beside her in the sunlight.

"See? I knew this would please you." Moving on top of her, it pushed her thighs apart to settle between them, and she didn't fight. It was pointless anyway, and it was in a good mood. That meant it probably wouldn't hurt her — not like she could stop that if it wanted to. "I only want to bring you pleasure right now, Danielle. To thank you."

The swell of her belly brushed the carved abs on the male form above her, and she clenched her eyes tight. She didn't want to think about it, about how long it had taken for its seed to take root. Two days in the real world, but it had felt like years in the dark. It might have been years of it toying with her, fucking her, wrecking her mind.

"Your mind is yours again. You know all that was kept from you..." It leaned down to kiss across her collarbone, inching down to capture her nipple in its mouth and suck. Tingles of pleasure zinged through her, drawing a soft whine past her lips before it released the hardening bud. "You know more than before... you *are* more than before."

"I'm still just your toy," she replied, deadpan, unable to even summon any feelings as she touched its human-looking skin with her blood covered fingers.

"Not a toy. A possession, a cherished possession." Another lopsided smile that looked charming on the face it wore, but she fought against the temptation to let go. To let it fool her.

"You don't cherish me. You own me like someone used to own those cars over there. I'm just something for you to use until you tire of me, and I look forward to the day you do." She stretched out on the soft grass, feeling the chill in the air and the warmth of the sun on her skin. All real. More real than the thing on top of her could ever be. "Then you'll finally let me go."

"My darling Danielle…" It chuckled, propping itself up with one arm so it could trace its knuckles across her cheek. "Forever is nothing to one such as me. Time is such a human construct, and as I feed more of my power into you… you will see it. You will understand that you are unique, and you are mine."

"I won't," she promised herself.

"You will," it answered. "And until the day you are finally changed enough to see past this petty humanity, I will show you my gratitude for freeing me by making you happy."

"You can't make me happy," she growled.

"I can, and I will. You are mine, Danielle, and always will be. I will simply give you the lie until you are ready."

"No!" she screamed, and then she felt a sharp stab behind her eyes, merciless and horrible. *Things were shredding, memories collapsing as they rushed past, stealing the air from her lungs as she screamed. Or… she could hear someone screaming, but they sounded far away. An echo. Something distant and not for her to worry about. She wasn't in pain. She was safe, and she always would be.*

Safe and whole and protected.

The headache passed, and she opened her eyes to the bright sunlight. She had to blink it away, shading her eyes with her hand as she sat up and turned toward the smell of smoke where a building burned. "Fire," she whispered, and she felt someone touch her and turned fast, yanking her arm back.

"No need to worry, darling. Everyone got out safely." He smiled, reaching over to touch her cheek. "Are you feeling okay?"

"I'm fine…" she trailed off, confused, because she was naked in a field, and so was he. And his name was—

"Christopher," he filled in, laughing. "You really must have been tired. Did you forget my name in your dreams, Danielle?"

"No," she answered, smiling as the fog of sleep lifted and she remembered them walking here to rest, to have sex in the shade of the tree. Safe because Christopher was with her, and they were meant to be together. "I'm sorry, I think I just got a little mixed up for a minute."

"It will be okay. I am here and I will always keep you safe." His hand rested on the swell of her belly, and he smiled warmly. "Both of you."

THE END

END NOTE

Well, lovelies, what did you think of 'Reign of Ruin'? Did you like it? Hate it? Come by the Dark Haven, or send me a message, if you want to talk about it. I'm sure you've got some mixed feelings about our not-a-demon friend... I know I do. Still, the 'Reign' world is something I really enjoyed writing in with its corrupt theocracy, post-apocalyptic insanity, and the never-ending options my brain has already imagined inside it. If you think you'd be interested in more, please tell me. I already have a devious idea about a particular angel that I think you might all like to meet.

Wanna meet him? You'll have to tell me, lovelies!

Until then, I thought you might appreciate a little *extra* about the history of this world, so I've written a short story called 'The Day the Sky Burned.' It's from Danielle's point of view, before she was taken, and I hope it feeds your curiosity about the possibilities here.

If this becomes a series, this 'Reign' world is going to be pretty dark and fucked up, but I've got my fingers crossed you're willing to walk that road with me.

Enjoy the story, lovelies!

Jennifer Bene

THE DAY THE SKY BURNED

SIX YEARS AGO

Tornado sirens were going off, blaring, but no one was running for cover. Instead, people were walking outside, staring up at the orange sky that looked as if it had been blistered. Mottled by strange clouds, almost... warped. Danielle had never thought about the shape of the sky before, not until she'd heard the shouts and stepped outside of work with everyone else to see the sky look *wrong*.

"What the fuck is that?" Kennedy asked, hands planted on her hips as she stared upwards like everyone else in the parking lot.

"I have no idea," Danielle replied, shaking her head as the clouds shifted, moving like they were pushed by a strong wind... even though their shape never changed. "Could this be some kind of terrorist thing?"

"If it is, we're fucked." Kennedy dug her phone out of her back pocket and squeezed the button on the side. "It's only 1:15, why the hell does it look like sunset?"

"Maybe it's a volcano?" Danielle suggested, and her friend snorted.

"You watch too many movies. Where the hell is a volcano anywhere near here?" Kennedy looked around at the other people in the parking lot, and Danielle followed her gaze. Everyone was on their cells, including their boss, Carter, and so she pulled hers out too.

She'd just tapped her mom's number, when an emergency alert started blaring, and she heard the same emergency siren sound coming out of everyone's phones around her. A weirdly artificial mimic of the real ones still wailing across the city. The little gray box popped up on her screen, but it was a short, unhelpful message: *National Emergency – Unknown Event. Stay inside until further information is available.*

An immediate explosion of conversation happened, more people filtering out of the various stores nearby, and absolutely no one was following the directions of the alert.

"Screw this," Carter said, walking over to them. "I'm closing the store. My kid's at daycare, and I'm not leaving him there for whatever this is. Go home, guys."

"Thanks," Danielle answered, and she grabbed Kennedy to drag her back inside.

"Wait, I wanted to get pictures!" Kennedy complained, and Danielle rolled her eyes.

"Take them after we have our purses, idiot. Didn't you hear Carter? He's closing the store early."

"Fine," Kennedy groaned, and they hurried inside. Danielle was trying her mom back to back, but she kept getting a *Call Failed* error. Sighing, she switched to text and tapped out a fast message to say she was going home. The little *Delivered* confirmation made her breathe a little easier.

There were no customers in the clothing store and so, as soon as they were inside, Carter shut and locked the doors. "Let's get our stuff and go."

It only took a couple of minutes to turn out all the lights and grab their bags, and then they were standing by the employee parking in the back, watching the sky turn a weird shade of reddish-orange. It looked exactly like sunset, except for the disturbing fact that the sun was high in the sky and still shining brightly through the strange haze.

"Don't come in tomorrow unless I call you. I'll text Bryce and Anne Marie so they know," Carter called out to them as he walked backwards towards his car. "Be safe!"

"You too!" Danielle called back, and she turned to see Kennedy taking pictures. Smacking her on the arm, she rolled her eyes again. "You're so fucking weird. Stop taking pictures of this shit. Go home and text me when you get there."

"Okay," Kennedy grumbled and dug her keys out of her purse. "You too. I doubt we'll have classes tomorrow."

"If the sky still looks like that, I'm not going even if they don't announce it."

"Ditto," Kennedy called over her shoulder as she climbed into her car, and Danielle waved at her as she did the same. The street outside the Westbrook Shopping Center was already packed, and Danielle got in line behind Kennedy's car.

Her phone vibrated and she grabbed it. It was her mom, and the text was simple: *I'm fine, on my way home. Dad is too. Can you get Mary? Love you.*

Sighing, Danielle inched her car forward and then tapped out a quick: *Sure. Love you too.*

Getting Mary would take forever with everyone on the roads at the same time, but Mary didn't have a car yet, which meant that she'd have to go by the high school and pick her up in the chaos. Switching to her text convo with Mary, she sent her directions: *Mom and dad are otw home. omw to you. Go to the pool parking lot off Hebron for pickup.*

People were honking, multiple cars losing their shit as traffic barely moved, and no one wanted to let anyone out of the parking lot. Danielle just groaned and sat back in the seat, shooting another text to her boyfriend, Christopher: *Hey baby, have you seen the crazy sky outside? I'm omw to get Mary and heading home. Text me when you get this.*

She inched her car forward, keeping the gap between her and Kennedy's car tight so some asshole couldn't cut her off. Switching to one of her phone games to wait out the traffic, she plugged in the charging cable. It might take forever to get Mary, but they'd be home soon, and someone would figure out what the hell was going on.

∼

Five Weeks Later

"Another burn spot, as officials are referring to them, appeared today over the southeastern part of Cordon County. Officials are reminding everyone that in the event of a burn spot appearing in your area, the best course of action is to stay indoors until it dissipates. Research is ongoing into the cause of these strange meteorological occurrences, but until more is known it's better to be safe than sorry. I know that's how my family and I handle it, what about you, Lauren?" The news anchor had a bright, plastic smile on his face, but Danielle could see the awkward way he held it.

There was nothing casual or smile-worthy about the sky burning, or… at least *looking* like it was burning. Like someone was melting holes through some kind of plastic version of the sky and then you could see a fiery sunrise through the hole. It was weird as fuck.

"Did you see that video online?" Mary asked, nudging Danielle with her foot.

"What video?" she asked, pushing her back with her own foot as they sat on either end of the couch.

"The one with the angel? Everyone's been sending me the link today. It's totally a real angel. The person who uploaded it said it appeared under a burn spot in Kentucky. Here, let me find it." Mary was already looking for it on her phone when their Dad huffed.

"It's not an angel, it's some asshole in a costume trying to get famous."

"Isaac!" Mom snapped from the kitchen, stepping into the living room to glare at him. "Really? Language. That wasn't necessary."

"I saw that video at work today. It's obviously fake. Special effects and CGI, and you two girls don't need to be feeding into the hysteria. It's not helping anything." Dad sighed and reached for the remote, but he paused when he saw the screen. "Sarah! They're interviewing Archbishop Dunne!"

Danielle sat up, listening as their dad turned up the volume and their mom walked into the room. The interviewer was off-screen, with Archbishop Dunne in the center wearing black, with a simple priest's collar at his throat. "Yes, I've been speaking with others about the subject," he answered to whatever had been said before they paid attention.

"And what does the Church have to say about the recent claims of angels walking on earth?" the interviewer asked.

"See!" Mary chimed in, turning to look at Dad, but he just shushed her, waving a hand as he turned the volume up on the TV.

"Well, while we know that angels serve God in Heaven, it takes a special circumstance on Earth for God to send one to us here. As the Pope said last week, we must all take stock of ourselves, our sins, and ask ourselves why God may be testing us and our faith." The Archbishop smiled, tight-lipped, as he stopped.

"Yes, we covered the Pope's speech on the burn spots. However, the reports of angels, and the videos that have surfaced, are pretty hard to dispute. Don't you think?"

"I think that seeing an angel is a gift of God given to only a few. If there are those who claim to have seen them, who am I to dispute their belief?"

"But, Archbishop Dunne, do *you* believe what has appeared in video? Have you seen the videos online?" the interviewer pressed, not giving up, and it was clear by the strained smile on the Archbishop's face that he was losing patience.

"I believe that God works on Earth through good works and good people. If, indeed, He has sent angels to walk among us, then I would stress the importance of following the guidance of the Bible in all things." He shook his head, still smiling. "We know that many of us have strayed from our faith, but in trying times such as these it is more important than ever to be vigilant. To stay strong against sin in all its forms, and to follow the laws that He set forth. *That* is what I believe, and I am sorry, but I do not have time for more questions."

"Archbishop Dun—"

"I'm sorry," the Archbishop repeated as he began to walk away, and the cameraman followed him. "I really must say goodbye. Thank you."

The camera shifted, focusing on the interviewer who looked red in the face as the sun beat down. "It seems that's all the time Archbishop Dunne has for us today, but I know many people are still looking for answers after the incredible videos we've seen appear online over the last couple of weeks. Stay tuned for further updates on *Angel Watch* with WXLA 5. Back to you, Ed."

"Can you believe that? They're talking to Archbishop Dunne about these crazies," Dad said, flicking the TV off with a huff.

"Sounds to me like the Archbishop expects all of us at confession this week. Not just me and the girls," Mom replied, giving their Dad a look before she wandered back into the kitchen to finish dinner.

"Ridiculous," Dad muttered, standing up to walk to the computer room.

"Here, watch," Mary whispered, handing her phone across the couch. Danielle took it and pressed play on the video. Quickly turning down the volume on the side, she checked to make sure their Dad hadn't heard the loud talking, and then watched.

It was shaky, clearly shot on someone's phone, as they took video of the burn spot in the bright blue sky. There was a central hole, and then a few other small ones around the edges. It was still creepy to look at, no matter how many times she'd seen them. The guys making the video were talking about it, and then someone shouted, "Holy shit! Look!"

The camera swung, tilted for a moment until it straightened out on a man walking across a field surrounded by trees. Huge, blindingly white wings extended out from the man's shoulders. They were so massive that it seemed like the sheer weight of them should knock him over, impossible for him to be upright. Then the wings pulled in, hugging close to his back, and the movement had looked natural. Not artificial, and the grainy image didn't seem like any kind of CGI Danielle had ever seen. It looked real… it looked like an angel.

"This is insane," she mumbled, still watching as the video shook again and slowly zoomed in on the angel.

"Keep watching," Mary urged, sitting up to lean closer, and Danielle shifted the phone so they could both see it. "This is the craziest part."

The angel took several steps forward, toward the guys, and they started freaking out. Backing up next to a truck, and the sound of someone opening the door on the truck preceded someone shouting, "Get in the fucking car! Get in!"

As the person holding the phone climbed in, showing the dash for a moment before they aimed the camera out the front of the windshield, another person shouted, "Go! Just fucking go!"

It seemed that the angel had stopped moving, but the quality of the video got worse as the person tried to zoom in further and then… it was gone. No flash of light, no movement of its wings, just gone. "What the fuck? What the FUCK?" one of the guys shouted.

"Let's go! Let's fucking go right—" The video ended and Danielle immediately started it over as Mary sat back against the couch.

"Crazy, right?" Mary asked, smiling a little.

"Do you think it's real?" Danielle looked at her sister and saw her shrug.

"I don't know… I mean, it looks real but, like Dad said, it could be faked." Mary shrugged and took her phone back as the video continued to play, swiping out of the app. "What do you think?"

"It's probably fake. It has to be." Nothing else made sense.

∼

ONE MONTH LATER

Danielle's head wouldn't be quiet even as she laid in Christopher's bed with his arm around her. He squeezed her tighter, pulling her closer, his exhale brushing over her ear. "Babe, you've gotta stop focusing on it."

"How can you think about anything else?"

"Hmm… maybe because I have a really good distraction?" He kissed her shoulder, her neck, and then he held her chin, turning her face so he could capture her lips. She gave in for a moment, sinking into the temptation to ignore the world outside for a little while, but she turned out of the kiss when his hand slid down her side.

"Christopher..." she grumbled, and he sighed.

"What is worrying about it going to do, babe? I mean, really, this is something the government has to handle. They'll figure it out and—"

"Are you kidding? They have no fucking idea what's going on!" Shifting so she was on her back beside him, she looked up into his eyes. "My mom agrees with the Pope. That this is some kind of punishment."

"That's such bullshit," Christopher groaned, rolling away from her, but she grabbed onto his arm before he climbed off his bed.

"How else would you explain it? All of it?"

"I'm not *trying* to explain it, Danielle. All I know is that it's fucked up and I don't want any of that shit to happen here." He sighed and shifted so he could lean back against the wall at the head of his bed, shoving a pillow behind him. "Look, I know your family is super religious, but they're going to find real explanations for all of this. It's just going to take time."

"Right," she mumbled, clenching her teeth so she didn't pick an argument with him. It was pointless. Christopher didn't even want to pay attention to what was happening, much less read about it or watch the insane interviews and updates on the news.

But, whether he wanted to admit it or not, the day the sky burned was a universal marker for every person on earth. Everything that happened referred back to that day. Every news report, every fervent speech from government and religious groups alike.

It had become *the* milestone by which everything else was measured.

There was nothing else that worked, because science was at a loss. Sure, they were still looking into it, and they had theories. Half-drawn conclusions that were all over the internet, the TV, and in people's mouths. Everyone was desperate for an explanation, an answer.

But the only answer that made sense was that angels were real… and they were very, very angry.

That had become clear with the attack on St. Louis. Survivors from the surrounding area had described it as a blinding light, a silent explosion that had vaporized the center of the city and left a burnt ring of destruction for miles around it. Some people had said they'd even heard a ringing sound as the cloud of ash and smoke and debris had filled the air.

If that wasn't God's hand… what on earth was capable of it?

Another question Christopher didn't want to debate or look into. She loved him, had loved him since they'd been sophomores in high school, but she definitely didn't like this side of him. Head in the sand, hands over his ears, refusing to even acknowledge the absolute chaos around the world. Other cities in other countries had been attacked too. No rhyme or reason. Just millions dead, an endless, tragic recovery effort — and more questions than anyone had hope of answering.

"Don't be mad at me," Christopher said, bumping her side with his leg. "Come on, babe, I'm not trying to be a dick."

"I know," she answered to the ceiling, feeling the twisting anxiety building inside her again. "I'm just looking forward to hearing what the President says. He's meeting with some key people that the Pope sent, and—"

"And you think that the whole *repent for your sins* thing is going to make whatever is happening stop?" he asked, clearly mocking her, and she climbed off his bed.

"A bomb didn't blow up St. Louis, Christopher! The government already said that."

"No, they said they didn't know what *kind* of bomb it was. That's different, and—"

"That's because it wasn't a bomb!" she snapped, growling under her breath as she turned away from him, walking to his desk chair to grab her purse. "I'm going home."

"Wait, come on, Danielle. Don't go, I'm sorry." He moved to the edge of the bed, hanging his legs over the side as he beckoned her back. "Come here, just lay down with me, I'm sorry I was an asshole."

Crossing her arms, she faced off with him, not moving any closer. "You *are* being an asshole."

"I know. You're right." He stood up and closed the gap between them, holding onto her hips as he dipped his head and pressed a kiss to her nose, and then another to her lips. "But I love you."

Huffing, she stared at him for a moment longer as he smiled and used his dimples against her. *Dammit.* "You're lucky that I love you too."

"Oh, I know. I'm very lucky and I want to show you just how grateful I am." He tugged her hips, walking backwards to draw her back toward the bed. "Think you can stay for a little while longer?"

"Fine," she said, unable to fight the smile anymore as he

pulled her down with him, immediately rolling her under him so that he could plant another kiss on her lips. This time she gave in completely, let go of the anxiety and fear and reveled in how good it felt. How good *he* felt against her. She could talk to Mary about everything else later.

~

SIX WEEKS LATER

"This is *His* judgment. No one can deny that anymore. Angels walk among us and they are bringing with them God's damnation of our society. We have strayed from His word, from the laws He set forth for us. We celebrate sin, bathe in corruption, mock the sanctity of marriage — it was only a matter of time before He punished us." The preacher on the screen was almost shouting, but it didn't deter the woman in another panel from laughing.

"You're ridiculous. Do you actually believe God is angry because women have jobs? Because that's what you told your congregation last week at your mega church, the one with a multi-million-dollar facility. I wonder how many homeless and needy people you could have helped with that." The woman rolled her eyes and the preacher grew red in the face.

"The Lord sees your sins and you will suffer for them, harlot!"

"Harlot?" She laughed harder, waving her hand. "Are you guys really giving this guy air time?"

"The only path to salvation for this world is to return to the laws set forth by Him in the Bible. We are approaching the end of this time of sin and we must do our part to ensure

God wins dominion over the earth, or we will all suffer under Lucifer's reign. We have destroyed the family by allowing divorce, by allowing woman — who brought us original sin — to abandon the home and take on the role of man. That is why—"

"You have to be kidding me! How am I supposed to debate someone this irrational?" she laughed. "The global economy would collapse without women in the workforce. We're so far beyond manly men swinging hammers for a barn raising. It might be a good idea for you to join us in this century."

"Good women will return to God as the promises made in Revelations show up on earth. We are already face-to-face with God's wrath, and we must act before we reap naught but destruction!"

"Good women? You mean women being subservient to men," she snapped.

"This is God's will. As it was set forth in Eden, so it should be on earth." The preacher raised his hand, like he was swearing a promise. "This is the truth that all of you refuse to accept, but the angels will make it clear to those still listening to God. We must act to save mankind. We must return to His laws. St. Louis, Ontario, Dallas, San Francisco… these have all been warnings, and we must listen."

The woman in the other frame threw her hands up, and then the anchor looked up from the pages on his desk with a solemn expression. "Unfortunately, that is all the time we have. Many thanks to Pastor Elridge and Theresa McDonald for their time today to discuss the recent comments coming from religious leaders around the world. Next up we'll have…"

Danielle pulled the headphones from her ears and sat back against the wall. Everything the preacher had said was still spinning inside her, bouncing off the more gentle sermon that their own priest had given at church on Sunday. While Father Thomas had not spoken of women the way the preacher had… there were too many similarities. The same concerns that we had strayed from God's laws, that the terrifying events were somehow God's anger showing itself on earth as it had so many times in the Bible.

Part of her wanted to brush it off like the woman had, but how else did they explain angels walking around? The missing women? The destruction of cities? The lack of bodies in the ruins?

"What are you sulking about?" Kennedy asked, dropping down next to her with a latte in hand and a paper bag.

"Nothing," she answered, locking her phone and tossing it into her purse. "Just waiting for my last class before I can head home for the day."

"I'm already done, but I'm going to grab a movie with that Luke guy."

"Seriously? A new guy?" Danielle laughed, and Kennedy stuck her tongue out at her.

"Not all of us found our one-and-only in high school. Plus, Luke is on the football team and hot as fuck. I think that's worth a movie… and maybe more." They both laughed, and Danielle stole a piece off of Kennedy's blueberry scone, even though her friend pretended to be irritated by it.

She needed to listen to Christopher's suggestions and stop watching every little thing that popped up about the burn spots, the angels, and the church's comments. It was just making her feel crazy, and that was the last thing she needed. She had the new semester to worry about.

∽

ONE MONTH LATER

"Mom, that's downtown, isn't it?" Mary asked, still staring at the television like they all were. "What does this mean?"

"Yes, honey, it's downtown, and I..." Mom trailed off, but Danielle could see the worry lines in her forehead, and she knew the pinched set of her mouth. Their mom was worried, and Danielle could see why.

The demonstrations and rallies had popped up over the last few weeks, but this one was here. Downtown, and based on the panning camera it was a packed space full of angry men. Hovering over the roaring crowd were signs saying things like *'God's Law is the Only Law'* and *'Serve Your Husband, Serve God'* and *'Women made Original Sin #NotAgain'*.

"I don't like this, Sarah," Dad muttered, and he looked furious as he glared at the television.

"We can't give in to fear. That's what we have to remember." Her mom reached over and squeezed Danielle's arm, patting it as she continued. "People do things like this when they're scared, but it will stop. The government will stop this."

A blue runner ran across the bottom of the broadcast and Danielle sat up straight. "Wait, is that *our* senator?"

Standing beside one of the self-proclaimed bishops was a man waving at the crowd, smiling. The text that ran across the screen said: *Senator Gramm joins The Church event.*

"I voted for that bastard," Dad growled, slamming the remote down on the little table beside his chair. Danielle glanced at her mom, waiting for the traditional correction of his language, but her mother didn't even blink.

Not a good sign.

As they started to speak, they were saying the same insane shit they'd been spouting for weeks. That it was the fault of women that God was angry, and the fault of men for allowing women to leave the roles God had meant for them. Bullshit about submission, obedience, service, motherhood. All of it ending in their rally cry... *God's law is the only law.*

"I don't like this," Mary mumbled, and Danielle hated how scared she sounded, but she stayed silent for the same reason Mom and Dad were silent. What comforting words were there for this? The fucking government was pairing up with these psychopaths referring to themselves as The Church. Capital letters, like somehow they were above the Pope now. Some of these men had been priests in the Catholic church, others had been preachers and pastors and reverends in other Christian denominations from across the country.

Actually, if it was just the United States it wouldn't be as scary... but The Church was spreading. Popping up in Europe and other countries, and people — men — were flocking to it out of fear. Promising to turn the tide on the chaos and destruction by *taking their women in hand.* It was like the whole world was trapped in some kind of fever dream, a nightmare that wouldn't end, that just kept getting worse. And now it was in their proverbial backyard.

"You need to quit your job, Danielle," Dad said, and she spun on him, shocked, but the grim expression on his face kept her quiet. Her mom brushed her arm again, squeezing, and she swallowed down the argument she wanted to make to listen to more of the insanity pouring out of the television.

"What do they mean by re-education, Mom?" she whispered, looking up at her mother who looked too pale. "Mom?"

"I don't know, honey." Another hard squeeze of her arm, almost too hard. The pinch of her skin hurt a bit, but she didn't pull her arm away. It was like her mom was leaning on her, and she couldn't deny her that.

The supposed Bishop Miller stepped back, and the next speaker was another pretender. Archbishop Flores, or so the blue stripe across the bottom of the screen said. Danielle's frustration grew as the man started to talk about original sin like it was some kind of sermon over Genesis, a pointed reminder that Eve first ate of the apple. That before Eve there was the traitorous Lilith, thrown out of Eden first for refusing to submit to Adam. And there lay his message, that women were either of the type of Lilith — traitorous, unfaithful, evil — or they were like Eve. Simply misguided, easily swayed to sin when under a weak hand, when left to their own devices.

Utter bullshit.

Absolute, completely insane, bullshit... but the men in the crowd were cheering. Shouting. Applauding. Chanting. And then they quieted to hear more as *Archbishop* Flores shushed them to share the worst news yet — they were partnering with the government to determine the best course of action to *appease God* and *end the attacks.*

"That can't be true," her mom said softly, fingers at her mouth, and then her father exploded.

"Senator Gramm is right there, Sarah! Right fucking there!"

Dad shouted, pushing out of his chair to pace the distance between the bookshelf against the wall and the coffee table. He kept glancing at the television, muttering under his breath. "Damn him, damn them all..."

"Isaac..." her mother whispered, and when Danielle looked up at her she saw tears in her mom's eyes and a sense of panic clenched her chest. Her dad was there in an instant, pulling her mom into a hug that ripped her mom's death grip from her arm.

"It's okay, it's going to be okay. I swear, Sarah. I won't let any of this happen, I promise." He rubbed her mom's back, turning them so he could look over her shoulder at Mary and her. "I'll keep you all safe, I swear."

~

One Week Later

"The FCC has announced today that all internet service providers, or ISPs, must adhere to the Congressional Decency Act passed on Tuesday. There is a deadline of thirty days to demonstrate adherence, and it is predicted it will result in the termination of service to over a million different websites currently available today. Dissenters are already filing suits in various courts across the country in an attempt to stop the implementation of the act on the grounds of constitutional violation." Ed Foster, the male anchor on the channel her parents always watched, glanced down at the notes on his desk, clearing his throat before continuing. "Another section of the Decency Act outlines new government privacy regulations which allow the monitoring of all communications as needed. Notices will be provided via letter from your ISP, cellular service provider, and any other telecommunications providers you may have."

"They can't fucking do that!" Christopher shouted, and Danielle shushed him so she could listen.

"High-ranking officials in The Church have been partnering with key members of Congress and the Senate in order to make decisions to protect the United States from any further assaults from the individuals referred to as angels." He paused for a moment before looking into the camera. "Since President Reed originally declared a national emergency on the day the sky burned, little has been done to use his emergency powers allowed under the declaration — other than to dedicate certain funding to the research of the burn spots and the alleged angels. However, along with the FCC's announcement, President Reed has announced today that any and all civil unrest in response to safety and control efforts implemented by the government will be dealt with swiftly through targeted military response."

"Oh, God..." Danielle whispered, reaching for Christopher's hand, which he quickly took, gripping it tight as they hovered in the doorway to the living room.

"We here at WXLA 5 want to encourage all of our viewers to stay in their homes this evening, and this weekend. We'd also like to remind our female viewers, especially, to stay safe due to the recent number of attacks on women in the metropolitan area." Ed Foster swallowed, glancing off to the side of the camera for a moment before looking back. "To end tonight's broadcast, I'd like to quote a great man by the name of Nelson Mandela. 'I learned that courage was not the absence of fear, but the triumph over it. The brave man is not he who does not feel afraid, but he who conquers that fear.' In that spirit, and in the spirit of our forefathers, I want to encourage all of you to be safe, but to also not sit back and let this happen. We must rise above the fear that has taken hold of our country, and we *must* fight it. We must not lose ourselves, and our liberty. The liberty promised to all of us, regardless of skin color, orientation… or gender. Do not go quietly. That is my message." He took a shuddering breath and brought his eyes back to the camera. "I love you, Amy."

The screen flickered, and then a commercial started for a truck, but neither she nor Christopher moved for a moment.

"Did he just…" Danielle's voice trailed off, and she felt tears burning her eyes as fear snaked like ice cold fingers around her spine and squeezed.

Christopher turned and pulled her into a hug, holding her tight, almost crushing the air from her lungs as the arm around her back became like a vise. "You're not going home tonight, you can't—"

The tears came, she couldn't stop them as she hugged him back, and his mother turned to look at them from her spot in the living room. Leann didn't move, but she sniffled quietly as she hid her own tears with swipes of her hand.

"I love you, Danielle. I'm going to keep you safe. I swear." His promise, whispered against the top of her head as he held her tight, only made her cry harder. It was almost exactly what her father had told her mother, exactly what she imagined so many men across the country were whispering to their wives, their girlfriends, their daughters. "It's going to be okay, babe. I won't let anything happen to you."

"I think…" Leann stood up in the living room and he released his hold on her enough to look at his mom. The woman looked at the floor for a moment, sniffling again, before she stood up straight and forced a smile. "I think you two should get married."

"What?" Christopher asked, just as shocked as Danielle was.

"It's just, I-I've been listening to what they've said, what they've been saying, and I think if you two are married then Danielle will be safer. With... with whatever they're doing." Leann nodded a bit, clearing her throat as she wiped at her eyes again. "You both love each other, and I think it would have happened in time anyway, but... things are different now. And I think your parents will agree, Danielle."

"I—" Danielle tried to make words form, but nothing in her brain was working. Words were stuck somewhere, jammed up, and she couldn't get them to move to her tongue to say them.

Christopher turned back to her, releasing her to press his hands against her cheeks, thumbs wiping away the tears as she saw his own eyes stretched wide, panicked. "Would you marry me? Will— *will* you marry me?"

"Honey," Leann said, so softly as she came around the couch to approach them. "I know you love my son, and I love you for it. You two could live here, I have the space, and—"

"But my sister..." Danielle said, half-dazed as she looked between Christopher and his mom, not knowing what the right decision was. She'd dreamed of marrying him... someday. But not now. Not yet. Not like this. Not when the world was on fire and coming for them, for women, for *her*.

"She's only, what, fifteen? I—"

"Sixteen," Danielle corrected the woman, swallowing down the acid etching her throat.

"Well, still, I don't think these re-education processes would be meant for someone like her. She's still so young, you know?" Leann smiled again, encouraging, and Christopher turned her face back towards his.

"Danielle, please?" He released her to drop to one knee, grabbing her hand in a fierce grip. "Will you marry me? I'll keep you safe. I swear, I'll keep you safe."

"Wait, take this." Leann ripped the gold band off her finger and handed it to Christopher, and he held it up. The scratched, weathered wedding band that represented Leann's marriage to the husband she'd lost, Christopher's father who had died of a heart attack the year they'd started dating.

Too much, it was too much.

"Babe, please, I love you. Just say yes. I'll ask your parents, I'll do whatever you want, I—"

"Okay," Danielle whispered, voice cracking as she nodded. Lost in a haze, feeling none of the joy she'd once imagined for a moment like this. "Yes."

Christopher pushed the ring onto her finger, and it stuck at the second knuckle, but he stood anyway and kissed her. Harder than he'd ever kissed her in front of his mom before, but Danielle didn't fight it, she needed to feel that connection. Something real, and Christopher was real. They loved each other. They'd always loved each other. This was just sooner than it would have happened, but it still would have happened. She knew that in her heart. She just wished she felt better, felt happy, felt *something* besides the bone-crushing fear that wouldn't let go of her as the kiss ended and Christopher hugged her again.

"I love you," he whispered into her hair, and she wrapped her arms around him and hugged him harder.

"I love you too. Always. I always will."

~

Two Weeks Later

"Kennedy, you should come here. You can sleep in our house, you'll be safer," Danielle pleaded, but her friend just huffed, laughing like there was nothing wrong in the world.

"I'm good at my apartment. I've got Snickerdoodle and enough frozen dinners to last me through the apocalypse. I'll be just fine."

Groaning, Danielle wiped her hand over her face. "Stop acting like this isn't a big deal, Kennedy! The fucking military is here, you need to be with other people. Not alone, by yourself, in what's basically campus housing!"

"And what do you think will happen if some asshole sees me loading up my car with shit to go to your house?" Kennedy blew out a breath. "Nah, I'm just going to lay low and—"

"My dad can come get you, help you load your car. They'll just think you're going home to your parents and—"

"Your dad is *white*, Danielle. There's no way in hell anyone is going to believe he's my dad."

"You could have a step-dad!" she argued, kicking the little plastic trashcan under her desk. "Please? Just let us come get you."

"I'm good, Danielle. I promise!" Somehow Kennedy sounded so positive, while Danielle was fighting back tears as she spun the gold band on her left hand. "They can't stay here forever. Didn't you hear what's happening in Pittsburgh? Total riots. People are burning the city down over there. They won't bother with the demonstrations here for long."

"I swear, Kennedy, I'm going to go over there and get you myself."

"*That* would be spectacularly stupid. You know they're stopping any women traveling alone right now, and—"

"Exactly! You don't want me to get caught up in this shit, so let my dad come get you. Please, Kennedy!" Danielle knew before she'd finished speaking that it was pointless. Kennedy had an iron will, and when she set her mind to something there was no moving her. That's why the soft laughter on the line didn't surprise her, even though it felt like something broke deep inside as her best friend started talking.

"I love you, lady. Really. But I promise I'm fine. There hasn't even been a patrol through the apartment complex, and I'm staying indoors. Just me, the quiet cat lady, not drawing attention from anyone." Kennedy sighed. "You focus on you, and your *fiancé*, and your sister. I'll be fine."

"You're so damn stubborn," Danielle grumbled.

"Ahhh, but you love me anyway." Kennedy laughed again, and Danielle felt her lips curve up in a smile, even though it didn't sink any deeper than the surface.

"I wish you'd gone home before all this," she whispered.

"Yeah, but my parents hate cats and I would have had to abandon Snickerdoodle with you, and you're allergic so... I'm here. But I'm talking to them every day, and once they can leave Philly they're going to come and get me *and* Snickerdoodle. They promised he could come with me."

Kennedy made a cooing sound. "And who is the bestest boy? Who's my little protector? You are! Brave little kitty boy."

"Snickerdoodle isn't going to stop them, Kennedy."

"I dunno, you haven't seen him when he's pissed off because I haven't given him his daily tuna treat. He gets damn feisty." Kennedy laughed, and Danielle wanted to scream again. To shout at her, but she also knew it was pointless.

"All right. Okay..." Danielle forced a deep breath. "You know you're my best friend, right? And I totally love you?"

"I know. You're so lucky to know me," Kennedy joked, and then she sighed. "But, yeah, you're my best friend too. We survived Algebra II together, remember?"

"Yeah, I remember. You saved my ass." Danielle leaned back in her chair, trying not to cry. "Just be safe, okay? Don't be a hero, don't do anything stupid. Promise me."

"I'm planning to be quiet as a church mouse over here. Quietly binge-watching my DVD set of Sons of Anarchy where the man can't tell what I'm doing with my electricity." She laughed again. "I disconnected my DVD player from the wi-fi after that last bullshit they pulled."

"Okay... just— shit, take care of yourself, okay? I don't know what I'd do if something happened to you."

"Same, girl, same. You better keep calling me. Tell me what the outside world is like! Is orange still the new black? I have to know." Another fucking joke, but it had been what made Danielle like her so much in the first place. Kennedy had a wit unmatched by anyone, and as beautiful as she was, no one expected her to be so damn smart. Biochem major with plans for a doctoral track. Before the sky burned, she'd had a bright future. Now? Now it felt like none of them had a future at all.

"I'll call you every day, I swear." Danielle stood up, knocking her desk chair back as she turned to wander around her room. "Keep your phone charged, okay? I don't want to have a panic attack because you zoned out on Jax Teller, all right?"

"I got it. Phone on the charger." Kennedy sounded a little more subdued for a second. "I do want to hear about what happens with you and Christopher, okay? Even though I can't be there, I claim Maid of Honor. Your sis can be second fiddle."

"Deal," she answered, unable to fight the smile. "I'll have Mary hold up a picture of you at the courthouse if Dad lets her go."

"Perfect. Then everyone gets to be blessed with my visage while you marry the first boy you ever took to bed." Another laugh that had Danielle rolling her eyes.

"Oh my God, you're ridiculous."

"Awesome is the word you were looking for, and you're right. I am." Kennedy was smiling, she could hear it in her voice, but she also knew her friend was too smart not to be scared. Everyone was scared, and what she wanted more than anything was to know for sure that Kennedy was safe — and that just wasn't possible.

"You're right, you're awesome. I'll call you tomorrow about the same time, okay?"

"Okay, talk to you then. Love you, girl."

"Love you too. Bye." Danielle hung up the phone, anxiety still thrumming through her as she tore open her bedroom door and walked downstairs. The TV was off, and she was glad, because she didn't need another reminder of just how fucked up the world outside was. She just wanted things to feel normal again. That's all she wanted.

∽

ONE WEEK LATER

Tom Ryland shuffled papers in front of him on the desk as the opening music of the news played, and then he smiled stiffly as he met the camera with his eyes. "Good evening, we have several stories for you tonight, but we're starting the broadcast off with an update on Executive Order 14127. As we mentioned on Monday night, this Executive Order outlines the new authority provided to the Divine Ops armed services branch, which have been distributed across the United States in metropolitan areas for the safety and security of the United States and its citizens. Due to the recent angelic attack in Reno, Nevada, female citizens may be selected for questioning and re-education based on personal or criminal history, or any actions observed by members of Divine Ops."

Christopher pulled her closer, and she glanced over at her father who was leaned forward, staring at the television intently. After a brief pause, Ed Foster's replacement continued.

"We would like to remind our viewers that it is important to abide by any direction given from members of the armed services, or local police. Refusal to submit to questioning is grounds for immediate removal to one of the re-education facilities outside the city."

Another extended pause as Tom Ryland cleared his throat,

tilting his head a moment, and Mary used that opportunity to move from the floor and squeeze between Danielle and their mom.

"Recruitment centers for those interested in joining the Divine Ops are available around the city, as well as all service locations for The Church, for those males aged eighteen and older. We are joined tonight by Bishop Wright, who will explain this opportunity and then lead us all in prayer. Bishop Wright?" Tom turned and the camera panned to show Bishop Wright in the white-collared suit of the priests they pretended to be.

Danielle turned away, burying her face in Christopher's shirt, and he immediately stroked her back, pressing his cheek to her hair as he whispered, "It's okay, babe. I've got you."

"Mom, what do we do?" Mary asked, and everyone turned their eyes toward her.

"We just keep doing what we always do. As long as school is still in session, you will continue to go, and I'll keep going to work, and so will Dad." Their mom smiled, leaning forward to hug Mary, but when her eyes met Danielle's… she could see the fear. The panic that she was hiding from Mary, and her father's face looked strained.

"I don't want to go to school anymore," Mary answered softly, muffled by their mom's shoulder.

"Honey, we can't have any truancy concerns, okay? You have to go."

"But Danielle isn't going to school anymore!" Mary complained, pulling back to turn and face her.

"Yes," their mom answered. "We withdrew her from college,

but that's fine. She can pick up her courses after this is all done, *you* have to keep going. Okay?"

"But I don't want to," Mary said, and she wasn't whining, Danielle knew what her sister sounded like when she was afraid.

"Dad is taking you to school before he drops mom off at work, right? That means you're escorted, and if anyone tries to stop you, then you've got a damn good reason to be there." Danielle reached over to squeeze Mary's shoulder. "Plus, if anything happens, Christopher can come pick you up."

"But you guys aren't married yet, they won't let him pick me up from school."

"We're working on that," Christopher answered, and Danielle just held onto the smile on her face. It had been almost three weeks since they'd applied for a marriage license, and there had been no response yet. What used to take two or three days, was now backlogged by too many people seeking the same protection Christopher wanted to give her. Leaning over her, Christopher nudged Mary's shoulder. "Plus, you're basically my little sister no matter what, right?"

"Not on the paperwork," Mary groused, crossing her arms, and their father suddenly stood up and stormed out of the room.

"Isaac!" their mom called, but Christopher stood up from the couch.

"I'll go talk to him," he said softly, already following her father out of the room.

"It's going to be okay, sweetheart," their mom said, pulling Mary back into a hug, and then she reached an arm out to pull Danielle in as well. "We will get through this. All of us, together. Okay?"

"Okay," Mary mumbled, and Danielle just nodded.

A few hours later, after Christopher had left to be with his mom and Mary had gone to bed, it was just her and her mom at the kitchen table. Staring at the patterns in the wood as they listened to her dad pace around the computer room, talking to someone on the phone loud enough that they could hear the rise and fall of his voice.

"Here," her mom said softly, pushing a glass of wine in front of her as she took the seat next to her once more.

"But I'm not twenty-one yet."

"So?" she replied, taking a sip of her glass before gesturing towards the one in front of Danielle. "You'll be twenty-one in three months, you're engaged, and... well, I don't think it matters much anymore. Do you?"

Danielle couldn't argue with that, and she lifted the glass to take a sip. It was cold, crisp, and she took another drink of it before she set it back on the table. "Thanks, Mom."

"It helps, trust me." A small smile tweaked the edge of her mouth before she drank again. "I want you to know that I'm glad you and Christopher are getting married. I think Leann is right, it will help."

"Not exactly the dream wedding, right?" Danielle asked, trying for a joke like Kennedy, but it fell flat.

Her mom took a deep breath, blowing it out slowly as she leaned back from the table. "You know, your father and I waited until we were married to have sex."

Danielle almost spilled the wine glass, saving it at the last second to settle it back on the table as she blushed with embarrassment and panic. "Um, well, I—"

"Don't worry," Mom said with a laugh. "Dad and I have known for quite a while what you two were up to, and we would have said something to you if we were worried."

"Oh…" Grabbing for the wine, Danielle took a larger drink, grateful for the subtle buzz that was already leaking into her veins.

"I remember being so excited before we got married. I was just, what… maybe six months older than you are now? God, it feels like so long ago, but I can still remember being so impatient." Her mom smiled, looking down at her own wine glass as she turned it around and around. "I wish you could have that. The nights with your friends as you're planning. The different dresses you try on until you find that perfect one… I would have loved to have done that with you."

"I would have liked that too, Mom," she answered quietly, stealing another sip of the wine as her mom stared at the table. Then she raised her head and smiled again.

"You're going to be a beautiful bride, Danielle. I know that your Dad is stressed right now, but he told me how relieved he is to know that Christopher is standing by you. That he wants to protect you, keep you safe. And Leann feels the same way. I think she's loved you like a daughter for a while now." Her mom sighed, drinking her wine before she set it back on the table. "We want you to know that you two can stay here sometimes. I know Leann offered her home, and I know her house is less crowded, but—"

"Of course, we'll stay here too!" Danielle answered, reaching across the table to grab her mom's hand. "I promise, okay?"

"That makes me so happy." Her mom let go of the stem of the wine glass to lay her hand on top of Danielle's, patting and then squeezing as she leaned closer. "He is such a good boy, you know? I'd always hoped you two would stay together. I didn't want to see him break your heart, and I'm just... I'm so glad he's good. He's a good man."

There were tears in her mom's voice, and Danielle felt her own start as she dragged her chair closer over the tile so she could pull her mom into a hug. "He is, he's a really good guy, Mom. He loves me, and I love him too."

"I know!" Sniffling, her mom leaned back, wiping her eyes and laughing softly. "I don't think I've doubted that for a while. But, you know, in times of trouble sometimes people don't turn out to be who we hope they are, but... Christopher has. For that alone I'd be glad to have him as part of our family."

"That will mean a lot to him, Mom. Thank you." Danielle wiped her cheeks roughly, sniffling back the tears as she sat up straight and her mom did the same. "Do you... do you think Mary is safe going to school? I didn't want to ask in front of her, but do you think we could just keep her home?"

"The school already sent out a carefully worded letter about truancy." Shaking her head, her mom reached for the wine again and took a larger drink. "It basically said we don't want to draw undue attention to ourselves. Do you understand?"

Nodding, Danielle felt that same cold tension clench her lungs beneath her ribs. It was a familiar sensation now, one that happened several times a day with each new flash of fear, each new moment of panic or shock or horror. It was almost more disturbing that it didn't stress her as much as it used to. "I understand," she whispered.

"Have some more wine," her mom said as she stood, walking back into the kitchen to grab the bottle out of the fridge and bring it to the table. "We both need it, I think."

As her mom poured, Danielle smiled. "Other than communion, I can tell you, I never imagined *this* happening."

Laughing softly, her mom shrugged a shoulder as she poured into their glasses. "Situations have a way of getting your priorities in line. Just don't tell Mary, okay?"

Nodding, Danielle raised her newly filled glass, looking at the way the kitchen light played off the pale golden liquid. "Well, this is to you then. I have the best family a girl could ask for, and I love you so much."

Her mom smiled, a real smile that she hadn't seen for too long. "I love you too, honey. So much."

They clinked their glasses, and then her mom leaned over to press a kiss to her hair. It was probably going to be the first time in her life that Danielle had ever been tipsy with her mom, or drunk depending on how much of a lightweight she was with wine… but she decided to leave out the times she'd drank with Christopher in high school, or their friends at college. This was something special. Important. And if it was the apocalypse, then who cared anyway?

∼

Two Weeks Later

Danielle was in her room, trying Kennedy for the twelfth time that day, when she heard shouting downstairs. Opening her door, she met Mary in the hall as they peeked down the stairs like they had as kids.

"What do you mean they took her?" Dad shouted, louder than they'd ever heard him.

"I'm sorry, Isaac. They came into the office, they had *guns*, we couldn't do anything. They made us stay in our seats as they escorted the women out. I swear to God if I could have stopped them, if they'd—"

"Where the fuck is Sarah?" their Dad shouted, but there was something different in his voice, and Danielle grabbed Mary's shoulder tight.

"Stay here," she whispered, and Mary nodded with wide eyes as she stood and walked down the stairs.

"I'm so sorry, Isaac. I swear I did what I could, I swear." There was a man by the front door, sunlight pouring in behind him, and Danielle checked the clock in the living room and saw it was barely after five. "Please believe me..."

"No, this is impossible. She's married! She's married to *me*!" Dad shouted, and his back hit the wall hard enough to make the pictures rattle. "Who took her? Who?"

"It was the military guys. The ones with the white crosses on their uniforms, th-the Divine Ops ones." The man grabbed onto her dad's shoulders, both hands fisting in his shirt to lift him. "You need to call them, okay? Call the number and tell them who you are, tell them who Sarah is. They wouldn't listen to any of us."

Mom? Danielle stood frozen on the last step of the stairs, and then the man caught her gaze and she saw the sadness in his eyes as he turned back to her dad.

"Isaac... Isaac! Listen to me, you need to call. Right now." The man shook him, hard, getting in his face as his voice grew more serious. "She told them she had kids. She mentioned

Danielle and Mary, okay? You need to call them. Where's the phone?"

"I'll get it," Danielle said, forcing her voice out in a croak. The landline was in the kitchen, beside the toaster, and she grabbed the cordless in a too-tight grip as she walked like a ghost back to the man she didn't recognize. "Here."

"Thank you," he said, harried as he grabbed it and forced it against her father's chest. "Isaac. Stand up, right now. You have to make the call."

Her dad took the phone in a weak grip, his gaze somewhere near the floor, and the man let go of him to dig in his back pocket. Yanking out his wallet, he produced a scrap of paper and forced it into Danielle's hand.

"This is the number he needs to call. He needs to explain who he is, that Sarah is married to him. Do *not* let him mention the two of you girls, okay?" The man's eyes drifted over her shoulder, and Danielle turned to see Mary on the steps. "Jesus Christ... *please* don't let him mention either of you. Just have him say that Sarah is his wife. Have him ask where he needs to pick her up, okay?"

The man turned back towards the front door, and she grabbed onto his arm. "Wait, where are you going? What happened?"

"I have to go home. I have to be there for my family, just... shit, don't answer the door, okay? Turn off the lights, pretend you're not home." His gaze landed on the ring on her finger and he caught her hand. "Are you married?"

"Not yet," she whispered, panic making her voice tight.

"Fuck." He laughed bitterly, releasing her to swipe a hand through his thin hair. "Well, it doesn't seem to matter anymore anyway. Make your dad call them, I have to get home."

"Okay." She nodded, and then he was gone, out the door. She shut it quietly, flipping the locks as she turned back to her dad, watching as he slid the last little bit to the floor.

"Sarah," he whispered, and she flinched.

"Dad, you've got to call this number, okay? You need to call and get mom back." Spreading out the crumpled scrap of paper, she read the numbers and then reached over to press the talk button on the phone in his hand. "I'm going to call, and you're going to talk, okay?"

"She's married… this isn't supposed to happen."

"I know, Dad. I know, but I need you to do this. Okay?" Danielle waited, crouching beside him, searching for a hint of her father's normal presence under the strange expression on his face. "Dad!" she shouted, and he finally looked at her.

"Danielle?"

"Dad, you have to call. You have to ask where you need to go and get Mom." The dial tone filled the silence, blasting out of the phone. It seemed too loud for the moment, and she felt her chest ache as tears brimmed in her father's eyes.

"I promised her this wouldn't happen."

Taking a deep breath, Danielle grabbed the phone out of his hands and then pushed him back hard. He knocked into the wall, looking up at her like he was confused for a moment. "Snap out of it, Dad! Right fucking now!"

Mary's gasp from the stairs echoed her father's huff as his eyes focused on her. "Danielle, you shouldn't—"

"Yell at me *after* you get Mom back." Danielle looked down, dialing the number before she forced the phone back into his hands. "Tell them who you are, explain you know they have Mom, but *do not* mention me or Mary. Okay?"

"Okay," Dad replied, barely there, but hopefully there enough for the phone call. Mary was crying on the stairs, and she shushed her harshly before turning back to her dad.

The conversation didn't take long. It was stiff, bureaucratic, but the information was given and soon her father hung up.

"They said they'll call me back."

Danielle nodded, trying not to freak out, to fall apart. Standing up, she pointed at Mary. "Go turn off all the lights, every one of them. Now."

"Why are you doing that?" her dad asked, sounding far away again as he turned to watch Mary race into the living room.

"Because they might come here. For us." Swallowing, she tried not to let the bile rise in her throat. "Mom mentioned us because she didn't want them to take her away, and her friend, the man that came here to tell you—"

"Blake," he filled in.

"Blake came here and told us that we should pretend we're not home. Just in case they come for me or Mary." Those words seemed to snap her father out of the daze, and he immediately grabbed onto her arm.

"No. They can't. You're my daughters, you're—"

"I know." She nodded, feeling the heat of tears tracking down her cheeks as she brushed them away. "That's why we're going to turn off the lights, and sit down together, and wait for them to call you back about Mom, okay?"

"Okay," he replied, so passive as she pulled him to his feet and led him into the dim living room. Dropping him in his chair, she set the phone beside him and waited for Mary to come back.

"I brought you your phone," she whispered, handing it over as she turned to look at their dad.

"Thanks."

"Dad?" Mary moved to her knees by the side of his chair, squeezing his arm as she spoke softly. "Daddy? Are you okay?"

Their dad patted Mary's hand lightly, absently, as he replied in an empty voice. "I'll get her back. I will."

"I know you will," Danielle answered, giving Mary a look that told her to be quiet. There were no more questions to ask, no more things to say. They just needed to be together. To be quiet, in the dark, and wait until they could get Mom back.

∼

THREE DAYS LATER

She hadn't heard from Kennedy in five days. Five long days, which meant she was probably gone. Just like Mom. Just like so many other people.

Just... *gone*.

A huge demonstration had resulted in violence just a few miles away the day before, people demanding the return of loved ones, demanding answers — but the Divine Ops had only answered with tear gas, and batons, and hoses. Hundreds had been arrested or hospitalized, although only two of the five local hospitals were still operating. The world was falling apart, and Dad wouldn't let either of them leave the house.

It was Sunday now. If Mom were home, they'd be at church. Their church, not *The* Church in any of its incarnations around the city. Although even Father Thomas had been struggling to create inspiring sermons in the face of so much horror. The congregation had shrunk, people abandoning the Catholic church for the monsters orchestrating the horror around them. A mockery of what she'd been raised to believe, a devastating reality that seemed to never end.

Dad walked around the house like a ghost, carrying the cordless phone like a lifeline, and Danielle did her best to keep Mary out of his way. When she couldn't stop crying the night before, Danielle had opened a bottle of wine and given her a glass, promising it was their secret, and then her sister had finally slept.

But Danielle hadn't.

There was no sleep to be had when every creak of the house felt dangerous, when every buzz of her phone seemed like it would be another death knell meant to break her. Christopher had come by every day, but he couldn't fix this any more than she could. Her dad had called the number multiple times, each time giving the same information, and on the last call they had only asked him if he had other women in the home.

Dad had hung up on them immediately.

Now, he was just empty. He'd found her grandfather's gun in the attic, along with an ancient box of bullets, and it sat fully-loaded on the table beside his chair. She'd already lectured Mary to never touch it, to leave it alone, but it also meant she was afraid to walk away from her father. Losing their mom had broken something in him, and he hadn't quite come back. He sometimes surfaced if the phone rang, or if Christopher asked him if he could take her to his house, but after he refused… he just faded away.

Not like she'd leave anyway.

She wasn't married, although Blake had pointed out that didn't seem to matter anymore. The Divine Ops would do what they wanted, and it was that thought that made it so hard to sleep. The ideas that skittered through her mind when she tried to close her eyes, when she thought of what they might be doing to her mom, to *any* of the women they had taken, it all made her sick.

Re-education. Punishment.

Words that carried a different kind of weight now that The Church seemed to be in charge.

Her phone buzzed and she glanced at it, grabbing it when she saw Christopher's name on the screen. Giving one last glance to her father in his chair, she took the phone call in the kitchen. But, as soon as she accepted, her stomach twisted.

Christopher was crying, unable to catch his breath as he tried to talk. "They came— they were here. M-mom opened the door. I told her not to, I begged them to leave her alone. She hadn't left the house at all in over a week!" Another sob, a broken sound she'd never heard that shattered something deep inside her as she slid down the kitchen cabinets, but he wasn't done. "They asked me if she was under my protection, and I didn't know what that meant! I didn't know what it meant!"

"What happened?" she whispered, trying to stay calm.

"They said I could join them, fucking *join them* and put her under my protection." Christopher groaned. "She said no. My mom told them no! She said that I was engaged, and they asked me if it was true, and I said yes! I — *Jesus* — I said yes."

"They took your mom?" she asked, trying not to betray the tears in her voice as she bit down on her lip.

"She told me it was fine! She told me to stay, to go to you, but you have your dad! Why did she do that?" Christopher was panicking, and she tried to take enough breaths to manage a steady voice.

"Christopher, where did they take her?"

"I DON'T KNOW!" he shouted, another sob breaking in before he sniffed harshly. "They said if I joined I'd know. If I joined I could protect someone."

"A-are you?" she whispered.

"What?"

"Are you going to join?" she asked, trying to sound neutral, trying to ignore the heavy weight of the golden band on her finger.

"NO!" he shouted. "I can't— I... do you think I should? Should I?"

There was so much uncertainty in his voice, and she clenched her jaw tight so she wouldn't let a sound slip past her lips, fighting the urge to cry as she sought the right words. "Y-you should protect your mom."

"Oh God... I can't. You, I can protect you."

She laughed, a bitter, hollow sound as she stared up at the ceiling. "I don't think you can, Christopher."

"WHY!" he shouted, but she felt it in her bones. Knew it was true the moment she'd said it.

"They don't want your mom, Christopher. They want *you*. They want *me*. For completely different reasons, obviously… but that's what they want. You should join to keep your mom safe."

"I can't do that, I can't—"

"You can," she urged, nodding and sniffling back her own tears as she pushed herself against the cabinet. "You can do this. Your mom doesn't have anyone else to stand for her. Just you, and they're not going to let you protect me."

"But I love you," he replied, a harsh edge to his voice. "We're supposed to get married. It's supposed to be okay!"

"I know." She nodded, looking at the kitchen table where she'd had that same conversation with her mother. "I know, baby, and I love you too. I love you so fucking much, but you know—" Her voice broke, and she tried to hold back the tears as she dug her nails into her thigh, through the pajama pants she'd been wearing for two days.

"Danielle…" he whispered, and she could hear that he was crying, and it hurt, but she forced herself to keep talking.

"You know they're not going to let you protect me. Not from whatever this is, not from wherever they're taking us." She sniffled, swallowing so she could talk. "My mom already told them about me, about Mary, and all I can hope now is that Dad can protect Mary, and—"

"NO!" Christopher shouted, a roar tearing out of him that made her pull the cell phone away from her ear as she tried not to lose it. "No! Fuck that, I'm not losing you. I won't—"

"You can't stop them. Not with me, and if you think about it… if you will stop for just a minute and think about it… you'll realize you know it too." She nodded even though he couldn't see her, her eyes searching the cabinets and the brightly colored towel hanging off one of the handles. "You know that the only good thing that can come out of this is if you join, which they might make you do anyway… but if you do it now, you might be able to save your mom. Get her on a list or something."

"That's not what's supposed to happen," he whispered, and he sounded as broken as she felt.

"I know…" She had to bite her cheek to hold back the tears for another minute. "I know, baby. But, no matter what, I love you, Christopher. I'll always love you. No matter what."

"I love you, too. I swear I love you, Danielle." He groaned, another choked off sob breaking across the line before he returned. "I will find you. I don't care what I have to do, but I will find you."

"Okay," she answered, because it was the only thing she could say when they both knew it was a lie. An impossibility. She didn't know when they'd come, when her house would be the one they knocked on, but… it would happen. Sooner rather than later. And, if she were lucky, maybe they'd let her father protect Mary. Pulling in a hitched breath, she spoke, "I love you, Christopher."

"I love you too, Danielle," he replied softly, and for a moment they just sat there. Listening to each other breathe in hiccups of air as she twirled the golden band around her finger.

"Goodbye," she forced out before she hung up and tossed the phone away from her. Not caring a bit as she screamed into the dark of the kitchen and broke down.

Sometime later, she felt Mary's arms around her, pulling her towards her as she sobbed, fist clenched tight around the ring that had almost been a wedding band. And that thought only made her cry harder.

∽

Two Days Later

There was an explosion next door, loud and disorienting, and Danielle stumbled from her parents' room with Mary on her heels. Her father was already holding the gun, looking out the remaining windows as he swiped at the air, wordlessly telling them to get down.

Screams and shouts came in through the new hole in the wall, echoed from next door. The Bells' house. Both their kids were grown, but Danielle hadn't been outside in so long that she couldn't even remember if their daughter had come home or not.

Had she?

Mary grabbed onto the back of her shirt, weighing her down as she guided them to the side of the staircase, hidden behind the couch from the hole in the wall, while their father marched from room to room.

Finally, he walked back to them, dragging Danielle upright with a rough grip on her arm. "Go down into the basement, I'll tell them you're not here. I'll tell them you're with Christopher—"

"No!" she argued, but he shook her, pushing her back into the wall, which made Mary squeak in fear.

"I will tell them whatever I have to so that they *leave*,

Danielle." He let go of her arm and cupped the side of her face, the anger leaving as he suddenly looked infinitely sad. "I can't lose you two. I can't."

"Dad, please…"

"I don't want you to come up, no matter what you hear. Okay?" He looked between her and Mary, yanking them both into a fierce hug, planting kisses on their heads before he pushed them back. "I love you both more than anything. It doesn't matter what happens to me, if you can run… you run. Do you understand?"

Danielle nodded, trying not to cry, wishing her mom was there, wishing that none of this was happening. "Okay," she whispered.

"Okay, Dad," Mary echoed.

"I love you," he repeated.

"I love you too," they both whispered, voices broken by tears as he grabbed the door of the basement and gestured inside.

"Hurry, downstairs. Don't make a noise." Their dad watched as they both moved onto the dim stairs, holding onto the rail as he leaned on the door. "Your mom and I have loved you so much. Remember that, okay?"

"Dad!" Mary shouted, but he shut the door, and a second later they heard the turn of the key.

Her sister started crying, but Danielle shushed her quietly as she moved her down the stairs, letting her sit on the floor at the bottom of the steps as Danielle stared at the door. Off to the side she saw the baseball bat, and she knew what she needed to do if anyone came down. She knew she'd fight, even kill to protect her sister. Just like her mom had, just like her dad.

All they had was each other and, in the end, that was all that would matter.

She had a family that loved her. She'd had Christopher, and Leann, and Kennedy.

It didn't matter what they took away, because they could never take them. Not really. Because that kind of love was permanent, even if it was buried deep.

Even if they hurt her, she'd remember that she was loved.

THE END

AFTERWORD

Not much to say after that, is there, lovelies? All I will say is that I really do want to hear what you think. I left off the short story right as she was taken so that you can use your own wicked minds to fill in the blanks that happened between that moment and the moment Danielle awakes in Eden for the final time. I wish you all the best in what you picture.

Want to share it?

Come by the Dark Haven on Facebook, or send me a message / email so we can chat about it. I really do have lots of other ideas in this world and I want to hear if that's something you'd want to explore with me! Thanks for giving this book a chance, lovelies!

ABOUT THE AUTHOR

Jennifer Bene is a *USA Today* bestselling author of dangerously sexy and deviously dark romance. From BDSM, to Suspense, Dark Romance, and Thrillers—she writes it all. Always delivering a twisty, spine-tingling journey with the promise of a happily-ever-after.

Don't miss a release! Sign up for the newsletter to get new book alerts (and a free welcome book) at: http://jenniferbene.com/newsletter

～

You can find her online throughout social media with username @jbeneauthor and on her website: www.jenniferbene.com

ALSO BY JENNIFER BENE

The Thalia Series (Dark Romance)

Security Binds Her *(Thalia Book 1)*

Striking a Balance *(Thalia Book 2)*

Salvaged by Love *(Thalia Book 3)*

Tying the Knot *(Thalia Book 4)*

The Thalia Series: The Complete Collection

Dangerous Games Series (Dark Mafia Romance)

Early Sins *(A Dangerous Games Prequel)*

Lethal Sin *(Dangerous Games Book 1)*

Fragile Ties Series (Dark Romance)

Destruction *(Fragile Ties Book 1)*

Inheritance *(Fragile Ties Book 2)*

Redemption *(Fragile Ties Book 3)*

The Beth Series (Dark Romance)

Breaking Beth *(Beth Book 1)*

Daughters of Eltera Series (Dark Fantasy Romance)

Fae *(Daughters of Eltera Book 1)*

Tara *(Daughters of Eltera Book 2)*

Standalone Dark Romance

Taken by the Enemy

Imperfect Monster

Corrupt Desires

The Rite

Deviant Attraction: A Dark and Dirty Collection

Reign of Ruin

Crazy Broken Love

Appearances in the Black Light Series (BDSM Romance)

Black Light: Exposed *(Black Light Series Book 2)*

Black Light: Valentine Roulette *(Black Light Series Book 3)*

Black Light: Roulette Redux *(Black Light Series Book 7)*

Black Light: Celebrity Roulette *(Black Light Series Book 12)*

Standalone BDSM Ménage Romance

The Invitation

Reunited

Printed in Great Britain
by Amazon